Copyright © 2015 Mark Fryday

The right of the author to be identified as the author of this work has been asserted in accordance with the Copyright, Designs and Patents Act 1988

All rights reserved. No part of this publication may be reproduced, stored in a retrieval system, or transmitted, in any form, or by any means, electronic, mechanical, photocopying, recording or otherwise, without the prior permission of the copyright owners.

Cover illustration by Grant Wickham
(www. grantwickham.co.uk)

Collapse of the Wave

Tales from The Red Lion Part 1

by

Mark Fryday

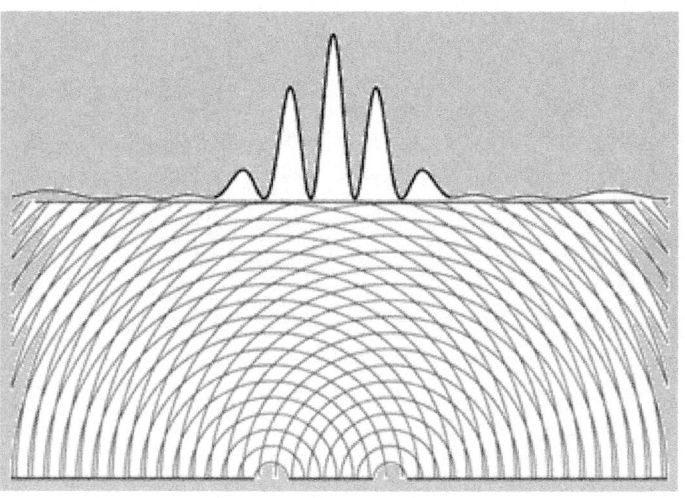

For Paul, Phil and Mike

Who made me make it happen,

and Oli C.

Who was there throughout,

and a constant inspiration.

FIG.1

fig.1 Electron gun fires electron towards the dual slits

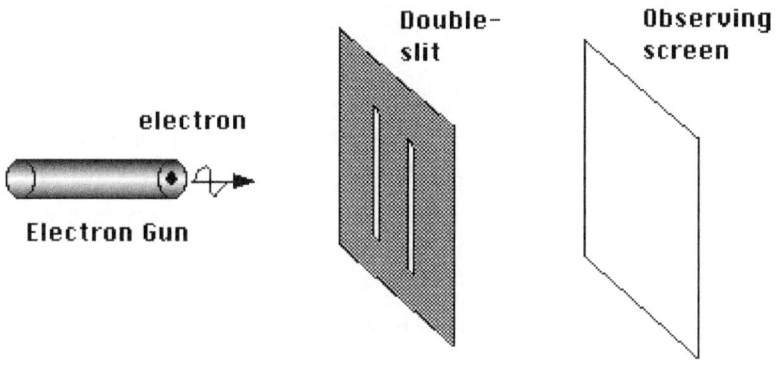

Forgive me.

"Forgive me, no this seat is not taken. Busy tonight, yes. Hang on, I'll just move my coat. Dan, yeah, nice to meet you too."
Shake hands. Make sure of eye contact. Not too much. Jess and Adam were good company as it goes, for this pub. But they were not really what I was after. Not tonight. Too comfortable and normal. Too happy. God knows what they thought of me.

I really do have to get to Dad's house now. I know, I'm just putting off the inevitable. Ted's got the story straight. I've now been seen.

And I had better go.

Chapter 1

Don't judge me, but I like a drink. That's not some euphemism for I've got a drinking problem. I just like a drink. It gets the conversational juices going, especially with us Brits. And a pint of beer is my thing. Whether it's the taste, habit, or subliminal marketing that dictates this I could not say, but I wouldn't have a fraction of the human interaction that I actually do have without it. Let's be clear. This is not a source of shame, or embarrassment, or anything like that. In fact, I'm a little proud, if that's the word, to have worked out some small part of this life that works well for me.

And so engaging in random conversations, while enjoying a beer or two, has been my thing lately, at least since I came back from London. After that thing with Mum. Sure, some of the old gang are still around but they're all busier compared to how we used to be from before. More often than not I usually end up down this very pub talking to people just like your good self and other sorts too, whoever happens to be there and in the mood for some kind of company. The fabled cross-section of society. That's fine by me. I feel more at home here than I do at home. I always get a little too introspective when I stay too long indoors. I know all my own stories and I don't need to mull over them again and again. And I would, believe me. I do. I'm working on the safe assumption that other people's stories are bound to be more interesting, and in here there's no shortage of people, after a drink or two, willing to part with some of theirs. People just love to talk about themselves in the main, and I'm generally happy to lap all that right up, whatever that happens to be.

You do get the beer bores of course, who are a relatively modern phenomenon. A mere generation ago we only had a handful of beers to choose from, mostly bland and underwhelming so I am told. Progress on availability of quality ales has been frankly outstanding, and I'm as happy as the next man, but these particular chaps can really be obsessive. They obsess about the myriad breweries, and the types of ale. They often take notes, which they compare with each other. They can talk for hours. Don't get me wrong, I understand where they are coming from. I am interested in all that stuff myself. But only to a point. I tend to restrict the findings of my research to 'I liked that' or 'That wasn't so great' and try to determine the kind of thing that works for me or not. I mean, it's impossible to remember all these beer names anyway and, more often than not, you will find a great beer just the once then never find it again. But that's ok with me. You just keep on looking for the next one. On a quiet afternoon, though, I can sometimes get stuck with some beer bores and, unlike my usual stance, have to extricate myself after a while. Beer is not life in my book. Beer is a way of looking at life. Don't get me wrong, I'm not criticising or anything. It's good to find something that you can be passionate about. I wish I could find that thing for myself, if I was honest, so good luck to them. Tell you what though, give me these guys over the wine bores any time.

There are rules, of sorts, in places like this. You can't just talk to anyone. Some people won't like it and some types of people I just don't like talking to. You have to learn to spot those. There are signs. The obvious one is the drinking too quickly, like it's a job to be done, rather than an experience to be savoured. Meeting someone in that mood will do neither party any good. That's ok, you can come to the pub to be alone, it is allowed.

Also, bear with me, you occasionally just get talking to someone who won't shut up. Occupational hazard for me I guess. I like to listen more than most, but you do need your conversational companion to take a breath at some point, even if only so you can direct the conversation about them in a more interesting direction. The best ones, of course, are those who listen as much as they can talk. Those are the rarest, and so are keepers, should you get the opportunity to keep them.

So, in summary, the pub can sure be a social minefield, but the risks are generally worth taking and I have come to trust my instincts when choosing when to start a conversation.

So, bearing all this in mind let me tell you about earlier when I was drinking with Stan. He's sort of a regular here, an alright sort of chap depending on what mood he's in. We don't always chat but we did today. Today Stan had a story. One that did not even involve his football team's latest dismal performance, thank goodness. We were firstly sitting wordlessly at the bar, him reading the back pages of one of the pub papers, me reading my book, having earlier exchanged the obligatory nod of acknowledgement. I was enjoying a pint of Number Two, which wasn't as bad as you may imagine. He was having one of the several lagers on offer. He eventually looked up at me and began, but not before the obligatory two pints, the ones that break down the default levels of British reserve. Once we got started, though, you couldn't stop us.

Stan tells me about his morning.
"So, I was heading off to Southend, down the A127 as usual, when my alarm went off, right…"
"Right. Unusual?" This was me, being interested.
"Yeah, of course. Why would you have an alarm go off in

your car?"

"Maybe in case you regularly fall asleep at the wheel?...joking! ...joking..."

"No. I know how to drive, man. I'm a bloody good driver. Made me jump out of my seat."

"Good job you had your seat belt on."

He ignores this. Fair enough. "It took me a minute to work it out. I was thinking maybe I had an early meeting booked up and forgot about it."

"That can happen."

"Wasn't that though. I was getting this nagging feeling. So I pulled off at the next exit and found a spot to stop so I could check my phone."

"Like you say, a good driver."

He regards me quizzically but carries on.

"Checked my phone. I put all my Calendar stuff in there you see. You do that?"

"Er, not really. Don't usually have that much planned."

"Anyway, turns out it's the wife's birthday. I'd already taken the day off ages ago and was going to bring her breakfast in bed, take her out for the day, and all that."

"Ah." Just me letting him know I'm still with him.

"So there's a couple of texts on my phone. From her. 'Where are you?' then 'Where the hell are you?' That sort of thing."

"So, let me get this right. You forgot your wife's birthday, and went to work on your day off?"

"Well, nearly. I never actually got to work. So I panic for a moment. Then survival instinct kicks in."

"Survival instinct?" I take a sip.

"You haven't met my wife. Yeah, so I send her this cryptic message, like I'm planning something secret or something."

"Nice work."

"Thing is, once I'd done that I now have to go and actually

do something. And I hate shopping. Bloody hate it." He swigs a decent gulp of his pint at the thought of it.
"This must have been pretty early though. No shops open?"
"Yeah, but I get this brainwave, right. There's this Waitrose on the way back. So I pop in there and get some flowers and croissants, and some posh orange juice."
"Posh juice?"
"Well, the bottle looked posh. Doesn't matter. Anyway, twenty quid and thirty minutes later I'm back in the house bearing gifts. She was pretty pleased, as it goes. I don't normally go in for such displays."
"Well you don't want her taking you for granted do you? Ha, what did she say when you told her what really happened?"
He looks me in the eye like I'm an idiot. I get that a lot. "I didn't tell her, did I? No chance mate. The…er… *alternative* version of this story works better for her, and much better for me, so that's just how it's staying. She'd never let me forget it if she found out I was driving off to work on her birthday! So, anyway, now she's been on the phone telling her sister about this lovely surprise and how maybe I've changed etc etc. I'm in the good books for once so happy days. Downside is I'll probably have to do the same next year."
"Who says romance is dead, eh?" I say.
"It's all too complicated this relationship stuff, yeah?" Stan asks me, I assume rhetorically.
"I'm with you there. Cheers."
"Cheers."
A pause.
"Er, shouldn't you be with her now then? It's still her birthday right?"
Stan checks his watch and says "It's alright. She's off down the hairdressers. Or nail bar or something. Then we're out for a meal."

"Wow. This is all getting out of hand."
"You're not wrong. Oh damn. I've still got to get her a bloody card. Said I'd left it in the car this morning. That's what I came back out for in the first place."
"Back to Waitrose then?"
"Yeah, well, in a minute." He swills the remaining beer around and around in his glass. "Thing is you know…I don't even like my job that much. What was I thinking?"

In return, I told him I had just got a beard trimmer, and that I had trimmed my beard this morning. I had never used one before, and I was pretty pleased with the results. It wasn't much of a story.

To me, there's something about a pub that allows this sort of thing to happen. I've never had the same feeling when drinking abroad. Bars in other countries seem to have defined purpose about them – drink this much, eat here now, dance over there - but a pub, or a good one at least, is content to just be there, and allow the visitor to make of it what they will. The key difference is that the pub wants to make you feel like you are at home, whereas a bar wants to make you feel like you are out. Being in a pub is like being in your front room, but with strangers in it. No, hang on, that sounds a bit wrong. Let me try again. It's like being in your living room, but with possibilities. And really nice beer. I've noticed that it's getting ever harder to find such places, year on year. I don't understand this trend towards the bland and the corporate. But I'm lucky. I have a few places to choose from and normally end up in this one by default. The Red Lion, where I began my drinking career all those years ago, and one of the reasons why I could even contemplate coming back home.

How would we describe the Red Lion? I have spent so much time here I suppose I take these surroundings for granted. There must be some reason why I come here more than anywhere else, but it's hard to quite define why that is. Let me see. It's not the colour of the wallpaper or the carpet. It's perhaps that there still is wallpaper and carpet, which makes the place look more traditional, from another time. Judging by some of the stains it probably is. To me it just seems *proper*. It has a proper bar, a u-shape smiling out to all corners of the room, inviting everyone to come forward for a drink, no matter where they are sitting. It has proper old tables and chairs, some of them more steady, or more sturdy, than others, which I find all part of the charm. Some of these chairs are like characters in their own right. It has proper beer, which goes without saying. What else? It has a pretty big chandelier, which I only notice once every ten times I come in here. I know. It has *history*. It has generations of stories and story tellers. It draws in characters. The bar down the road, busy as it is, contains none of this for me.

Stan heads off, maybe to Waitrose. Then, a little later, I somehow ended up talking to this guy from the Aleutians. That's the Aleutian Islands, I found out, when I looked it up later. He chases bears out of town amongst other things. Not for a laugh. He is a State Trooper or something. I found it a little mind-blowing how he managed to travel all the way around the planet, when he could have gone literally anywhere, and ends up here talking with me. But I did not tell him that, I mainly just listened a bit. He lives in such a small town that there are not even any shops, just air drops. So he needed a change of scene, he said. Fair enough, I said, we do have some shops here after all. I then said that I needed a change of scene too so perhaps I should go there. He laughed. He's right. I know that I won't. Kids as young as thirteen carry guns over there, he told me. I did not know what to say to that so I sipped thoughtfully on my pint and asked him about the flight. It was fine. You sure can learn a lot in here if you go about things the right way.

Don't worry, this is not turning into some story of some English hero who moves away out of his comfort zone to battle rogue bears and gun-toting kids. A shame possibly, but no, it's not that. Anyway, after a while, he was gone. Perhaps to go shopping too. It was turning into that sort of day. Good luck to him.

Of course, you don't always have to chat. You can just overhear a conversation if you wish. It might be a bit rude but if someone really wanted to be secretive they wouldn't talk here right? There are rules around this too though. Sorry if I'm bombarding you with rules, but I want to make sure you feel comfortable. The thing is here, if the conversation gets too heavy you really should try and tune out, or subtly move off, pretending you desperately need to be somewhere else all of a sudden. After all, sometimes people can't control the moment, especially after a few. Another rule is that if you do happen to be eavesdropping, whatever you do, don't *look* like you are eavesdropping. That way everyone can feel comfortable in the pretence of privacy. Therefore you can't eavesdrop unless you are on your own. Otherwise that would look too weird. It would also *be* too weird. Then, once you have established that you are, in fact, on your own, you should always have some form of generally recognised distraction, like a book, with you. Good boozers also have papers that you can pretend to read too. Beer mats do not generally constitute sufficient reading material, let me tell you.

So, once the state trooper has gone I begin earwigging a conversation on the next table. That's ok, I am evidently engrossed in leafing through the financial section of The Times, which was handily left near the bar, unwanted. Two women are talking. It's still early and they are the only women in the pub. They are sharing a bottle of white wine. I couldn't tell you which wine it was. Sorry, but if I leant in any closer it would blow my cover. Imagine it is a Pinot Grigio if you must. One of the women is angry, the other is mainly listening and being sympathetic.

"So I told her."
"You told her? Really?"
"Well, that's the point of an exit interview right? Get everything out in the open. Say your piece and move on."
"I don't know. You don't want to burn your bridges."
"Screw that. I'm never going back there. So I told her."
The man at the next table, that being me, is now suddenly curious to know what she actually *did* tell her.
"So what did you say then?"
Good question.
"I told her just what I thought."
Oh come on.
"She deserves it. She's been such a bitch to you since she got promoted. Everyone says so. Like she's so jealous or something."
"Tell me about it. It's only because Ed knocked her back at the Christmas party. She knows he likes me and she can't handle it. So she's been sniping at me every chance she got. And giving me the duff jobs. How was I going to hit my targets with that lot?"
"Oh, I know. She's such a bitch. She always was, you know."
And this bitch was told *what*, exactly? I noisily turn the page of my paper, to emphasise the fact that I'm not listening.
"I made sure she saw me give Ed my number when I was on my way out too. That showed her."
"I know, you should have seen the look on her face.

Everyone saw."
"That'll teach her."
Hey, you can't just jump off to that bit. What about..?
"Hey, but what if Ed actually calls you?"
"No problem. I might give him a quick go. Especially if she was going to find out."
"Oh, she would, don't you worry, she would."
"Hmm, this wine's a bit rank."
Jesus!
"Yeah, it's way better in Corkscrews up the road. Don't know why we came in here. There's no one here anyway either."
Er…
"Let's just neck these and head on."
"Uh huh, down the hatch. Up yours, Janice."
I put the paper down and head to the bar. Hey, I never said eavesdropping was always a good idea, did I?

So you could think of all this as a typical kind of day. I don't like to talk about myself much and living like this I don't have to. I don't even like to think about myself much either, now I think about it. So I'm happy to just drift for now, *determined* to if that's the right word.

Since we're here though, if you don't mind, I suppose I could tell you this little something. You might know this sort of picturesque field on the way to the pub, yeah? Just before the crossing, I sometimes stop there to cleanse my soul as it were, or calm me down. Like counting to ten, but with a view. It's just a rather flat nondescript piece of land, which will no doubt end up just being flats shortly, but often has some kind of different flower or other blooming on it most of the year round. I find it provides the eyes with some sense of space, some… perspective. A chance to relax the eyes from the close focus of the streets and the constant distraction of the ever-increasing advertising.

Always for things I don't want, I find. Anyway, I often feel a growing sense of contentment while standing there. But, despite this, something is always trying to pull me away when I stand there. Boredom, or embarrassment, or the need to do the next thing will always gnaw at me until I find myself walking down the road again, not sure why the decision to move on was made. Or who by. Well, I know who by because I was reading about that the other day, but I might get to that later. Today, today I walked away because of the rabbit.

You see, you often see rabbits there. I wouldn't go on about this sort of thing down the pub normally, but I confess that those little guys always make me smile. It's satisfying to see an animal going on about its business in its natural habitat. Joyful even, if I'm in that sort of mood. Sometimes I pretend to wonder if the rabbits feel the same about me as I head down the road, but that's just for my amusement, because they don't, I'm sure. They are just there, chomping away on the grass and avoiding being killed for another day. Sounds like a temptingly simple lifestyle compared to the complexities running around my head. Without the being killed bit.

But life was not so grand for this particular fella. It took a while to sink in because he was just chomping away as usual. Then he walked into a tree and then tripped on a discarded can of lager. And then I saw the eyes. All red and mostly closed up, turning the face sad and ugly. My heart / stomach does that somersault thing. That means various glands are sending out combinations of unwanted hormones, which are now flinging themselves around my bloodstream, making me feel things. Myxomatosis, I recognise. In the rabbit, that is. One bastard of a disease.

Get this. It was only discovered in 1896 in South America, in imported rabbits. So, you see, humans are getting involved here already. Then full marks to Dr Delille who, in 1952, deliberately introduced it to his estate in France to get rid of the rabbits there. Within a few months the disease had spread across the region, but he blamed poachers. I couldn't find out if he was working on a similar solution for dealing with them. By 1955, and with the help of some delightful individuals deliberately placing sick rabbits into healthy burrows, 95% of rabbits in the UK were dead. Fast forward to this little guy, who is no doubt going to have a sorry few days before 'avoiding getting killed' is no longer an option.

Yes, I did do a little research on the subject. It makes you realise again what a fragile world this is, and how fragile we are within it. Back at the field, I couldn't deal with that thought. The legs started me moving again well before the boredom or embarrassment kicked in, and I left the poor rabbit to it.

Rant over. Moving on. Don't want to spoil your day.

Chapter 2

When I'm not down the pub I am often seeing Dad these days. He's the main reason I am back after all, now that he is on his own. That and the thing with Jen I suppose. We went for a walk by the river today, since the sun is out. We get on pretty well, always have. Now I'm older I can see how I may be becoming more and more like him. Or so it seems, it's hard to be sure from here. We often chat about the books we are reading and today find a nice spot on a grassy bank after a while. He's still pretty fit but I've noticed he likes to take a rest more often than he used too. It used to be me wanting to first find a spot to sit down. These days I always feel just so restless that I find it hard to stay still for too long. We are staring at the sky, enjoying the sunshine. Dad's name is George, just so you know.
"Eight minutes and 20 seconds," he says.
I turn to look at him. This is not a reference to the length of our stop-over. He's going to make me work this out. We've been doing this since I was six.
"Eight minutes and twenty seconds," I repeat, slowly, to buy me some time.
He turns to look at me. "Clue?"
He'd love that, but I can feel my brain pulling up something from under the surface of my memory. I just need to relax and buy a little time. "No thanks. I know this one."
"As you wish. Lovely day, for once. So bright."
"Shush." I'm getting there. Got it. "Light from the sun. Eight minutes and twenty seconds. The surface of the sun to my retina. 93 million miles."
"On average. Could be less, could be more."
"On average. Good enough?"
He looks pleased. "Oh yes, I thought I might have had you

there."
We look up for a while. He lobs in another thought.
"Light is made of photons."
"Yup."
"And photons are particles, right?"
"Yup again."
"But all the colours we see are light of different wavelengths, so light flows in waves. So what is it? Particles or waves?"
Oh right, it's going to be one of *these* walks. As hard on the brain as on the feet. I just sigh and hang my mouth open. Classy.
"I've started reading that book on Quantum Mechanics you lent me," Dad explains. "It's rather thought provoking so far."
I had forgotten that I had lent him that book. It must have been months ago. That was probably a mistake, thinking about it. I just say, "Crikey, it was fun to read but most of that made no sense to me at all."
"I don't think it makes sense to anyone, as far as I can gather. It seems best to just run with it. It works, you just get tied up if you try and explain it."
"That is hardly the scientific method," I say. I'm no scientist, by the way, but I am sometimes an amateur enthusiast, as is Dad. We've been conversing this way for decades now, since my first obsession with astronomy.
"True," Dad concedes, "But one step at a time. Think about it. For the sub-atomic stuff there are practical difficulties. For bigger particles you can bounce light on them so we can have a look and the light does not affect it enough to change it. Right?"
OK, I get that. "Right."
"But you can't shine a photon on a photon without them just bouncing off each other, can you?"
"...and never getting to the retina of the observer. Yes, that

rings a bell."

"So we have to rely on other methods of detection or work out probabilities of where these particles are. We can't know for sure where they are or are travelling lest we change where they *are*."

"Problem." I admit.

"Hmm, anyway, I've just got started really. I'll report back next week."

It's been a while since I read that book so I can't remember if this is even right or not. Rings a bell, but it might be a bit of a simplistic summary. I should re-read that when he gives it back to me. For now, though, think I need to change the subject. "You know, you used to say that of me, Dad. When I was younger. 'I never know where you are', you kept saying."

He smiles. "Always out you were. Straight after tea. No mobile phones then, either. It was like you jumped out the front door and just disappeared off the face of the earth."

"Ha. We *did* sometimes, or imagined we had. Flying into space in a cardboard box! I was only ever a street or so away though. Just hanging around or kicking a football usually."

"Yes, yes, but you worry when you're a parent. You never stop worrying. I'm still worried! You yourself may find this out one day."

"Hmm, don't hold your breath."

A pause. I can't just magic up a relationship again, just like he can't. We ponder our mutual positions (or superpostions, ha ha) in silence for a moment. If I remember correctly, a sub-atomic particle can be in two places at once, sort of, so is said to have a superposition. I wonder if there's a version of me out there in another position, with a wife and kids, being a normal functioning member of society or whatever. I wonder if there's a Dad out there who still has Mum to walk with on days like this, instead of me. I keep these

thoughts to myself.
Dad speaks first. "I would like some grand-children I may actually like."
This change of subject is not going to plan. I pull the conversational emergency cord.
"Ok, ok. So…how did the football go on Saturday?"
He eyes me up and raises his eyebrows. "If you actually cared you would know already, but since you ask…"
He carries on for a while but I can't remember the details. I can't retain football-related facts. It's most likely because I just don't care enough. Dad, and many people I know down the pub, seem to be savants on the matter. Some blokes don't seem to know much at all about the rest of the universe, as if their brain is so full of football statistics that there is no room for anything else. They often seem happy enough though, so I'm not going to judge. My brain works the other way. It is always too full of all that other stuff out there to hold onto sporting statistics. I close my eyes and let Dad's words, and the sound of his voice, wash over me, along with the heat from the sun. It is safe and comforting, for a while.

He sometimes talks about Mum, but not today. After a while I head off, after arranging to meet up for his birthday later that week.

Not long after, I was down the pub, where, while waiting for Amy, I ended up talking to Koachi Gazan. You don't know him. He's the sort of bloke that always looks effortless in a strange pub, affecting the sort of comfort that usually takes me years. Blue jeans and dark glasses. He is up from London for the week. He doesn't live in the same part of London where I used to live though. Some other place. He had family stuff to do up here, but he wasn't specific. He asked me if this was the best pub in town. I assured him that this depends entirely on your point of

view, not to mention your current mood.
"And what is your current mood?" he asked.
"Thirsty." I replied.
And that was that. He gets a round in and we start to chat about whatever. After a couple more pints, trips to the Gents predictably ensue and I notice that whenever he stands up he always put his hands in his pockets.
"This isn't London you know. No one is going to nick your wallet from your pocket in here."
He looks back at me quizzically but he's already on his way, his muscles already relaxing no doubt. No going back from that, for sure. You've just got to carry on. Fair enough.
On his way back, he holds up his hands in the air and smiles at me.
"Hope you washed them." I said.
"Naturally. And you have an excellent hand dryer. Very fast."
"That's the main reason I come here."
"Ha. I agree. A very important thing some landlords forget about, yes?" He looks at his hands. "My hands? My hands, I know."
"Always in the pockets?" I check. Things can digress very easily at such points in the evening.
"Well you have to put them somewhere."
"You do. You do that." I nod sagely. Or a close approximation of such.
"And I shall catch less germs in there than out here."
"Not with my trousers." I assure him.
He laughs. I wasn't actually joking.
"But I also do it to look cool. Why not?"
"Why not. Cheers." I say and offer him my glass.
Clink.

A little later, getting brave, I try and see past the dark glasses into his eyes, but the light in here and the shade of the lenses somewhat prevent this. That puts me off my stride normally, not being able to see people's eyes. That's the best bit of a person, more often than not. This may be one reason why I prefer winter, since hardly anyone wears sunglasses then. There are probably more reasons though. Anyway, the habit of wearing sunglasses indoors has always bugged me, especially on the Tube for God's sake. I know I shouldn't ask, but I am sufficiently drunk now to enquire of Koachi Gazan, perhaps a little too haughtily, why he has to keep his on in such a dingy boozer.
"Trying to look a little extra cool eh?" I suggest.
It turns out that both he and much of his family have a rare eye disorder that causes some discomfort in bright light, and a potentially disconcerting eye discolouration.
Sometimes I need to listen to myself and keep my mouth shut.

After a brief moment of silence, and a sip, that is exactly what I say to him. He laughs.
"Possibly so. But I *do* look cool, yes?"
I had to agree, and bought him another pint. While we are supping on that one we can't help but overhear a couple of blokes at the bar, speaking loudly enough to be heard from across the whole pub.
"I'm not racist…"
"I know, mate, I know you're not…"
Koachi Gazan looks over to me and raises his eyebrows.
My eyebrows return the favour.
"I'm not racist,…"
There's always a 'but'. Here's the 'but'.
"…but they never pour you a proper pint right? I mean I'm paying for a pint, so I want to *get* a pint. Am I right?"
"You're right, mate, you are right."

"Some of them must just have halves or litres or whatever and they don't know that a pint means a pint. I don't want half a glass of head do I?"
"You don't. 'Cept maybe that's ok on your holidays."
"'S'pose. Maybe. But if they come over here and want to get our jobs and work in our pubs they need to learn how to pour a proper pint."
"Right."
"And speak English."
"Too right."
And so on. Koachi Gazan and I are sitting a safe distance away so can discuss this supposition at a comfortable volume level without risk of detection.
"Sorry," I begin. "This is not the most cosmopolitan town sometimes."
"That's ok. There are still many like this in London. I would find the same back home also. Us human beings, we are bound to be… what is the word?"
"Idiots?"
Koachi Gazan chuckles politely at this. "Ha. No I mean like bound together but apart."
"Er…tribal?" I offer after a moment's thought.
"Tribal! Yes, that is the word. Tribal. Thank you. Safety in the group."
"I'm not part of that tribe," I assure him, nodding over to the brace of blokes.
"I know. I can tell this."
"I'm not part of any tribe really."
"No?" Koachi Gazan enquires.
"No. I don't think so. Bit of a lone spirit, me."
"But you drink in here, yes? And not so much in another place. This is tribal."
"Hmm, ok I may grant you that. Maybe a little. I never thought about it in that way before."
"Well, I am glad I came here and gave you a new thought. I

like to do this at least one time every day if I can." Koachi smiles at me, like I've made his day.
"You're welcome. If it is a tribe, it's a very loose one," I continue. "A tribe of similar strangers."
"Yes!" exclaims Koachi Gazan, patting me roundly on the shoulder. "Similar strangers. I would join that tribe."
"Welcome in," I say. "The password is 'Cheers'."
"Cheers!" We chink glasses.
"I don't even know what his problem is," I say, nodding to across the pub. "The landlord just served him that pint, and he grew up three streets from here."

Before Koachi Gazan leaves I let him know he is always welcome back here, provided he remembers the password. Shortly after he has gone, I get a text from Amy saying she had been sitting in the back bar but had got sick of waiting for me, so had gone off for some dinner. Will see me later. She can't have looked that hard though. Maybe she just saw Koachi Gazan here at the bar and missed me entirely. I can forgive that. The brain just can't take everything in, you see, it just fools you into thinking it does. Ah well, shame they didn't meet. She might have liked him. Half a pint later, this got me to wondering how many of those crux moments in your life, the real turning points, come and go without you ever knowing they were there at all. Like when you choose the wrong way rather than the right way or, more likely for me, never choose anything at all. I wonder, if you could be given a spreadsheet of all those really important moments in your life, with the moment in question in one column, and whether you made the right choice or not in another column, would you really want it? A sneaky peek even? No, you'd never want to see that list would you? The column of wrong choices would be too long a list to bear, surely.

With this thought in mind I look at the door. Perhaps the love of my life is walking past right now and if I don't leave immediately I shall miss her forever. Shut it, Dan, you idiot, I think, and turn back to the bar. That's never going to happen.

Then in comes Amy, her mouth all smiles and ketchup. I'm on an empty stomach. This could get messy. Turns out she did notice Koachi Gazan earlier after all.
"Thought he looked pretty cool for this pub," she says.
We both leave that to sink in for a moment. Once I'm aware that this is all she is planning to say I start things up again.
"Yes, and I was standing right next to him," I assure her.
To the untutored eye, she then looks like she's considering an apology. But we are way beyond such niceties in our relationship, so she's only pretending. The look is enough for me anyway.
"Well, you do come in here to hide, don't you?" is what she actually says instead.
"Er, hello?" I wave at her with both hands. "I'm here. Look at me, right here."
She sighs, like she has to explain something I should know already. Which is true. "Yes, but you sit back and watch don't you. You hide in the crowd…"
"Crowd? In here?" I gesture around to the empty tables.
"Whatever. What I mean is, you don't *project*."
"I can project…"
"The other fella…"
"Koachi Gazan."
"As you say, Koachi Gazan. He was projecting. He was making the whole room aware of him, just by the way he stood there. You don't do that."
I don't do that, this is true. "Hmm, sounds like you are just trying to make an excuse for missing seeing me." I

conclude.

"Nope. So therefore…my conclusion is that you come in here to hide. You let the others take attention and just watch the proceedings. You like to dissolve into the background."

"Is it this jumper? I ask, showing off my jumper. I'm not going to describe the jumper. Use your imagination.

"No, but hold that thought. I like that in you Dan. You're not a peacock. God knows I meet enough of them."

"Koachi Gazan wasn't a peacock. He was a nice fella…. anyway, what's wrong with the jumper?"

"I meant hold that thought for later, not grip it tightly and don't let go." Amy is not as exasperated as she may sound to the eavesdropper. She loves this really.

"How much later?" I like to wind her up too. These things have to be mutual or they're not so much fun.

"Right, that's enough. Drink up. We're going clothes shopping. You need at least one semi-peacock outfit or I may never be able to spot you in here."

"Shopping? Jesus, Amy. I thought you were my friend!"

"I am. Only a true friend would do this for you."

"So why have you got that look on your face then?"

"What look?"

"Er, evil Bond villain. *That* look."

"I've worked hard on that look, it would be a shame to waste it. Anyway, just because this is a job that you need doing doesn't mean I can't enjoy it too."

"I'm not going."

Of course, we do go. But we compromise. We go after the next one.

The family is going to be all together for Dad's birthday. With one exception of course, but we shan't mention that. I thought that Rachel, my sister, might have invited us over to her house but she was 'up the wall' so we decided to meet in a restaurant, somewhere mutually convenient for both of us. Rachel ended up making the final choice in the end, and despite some other suggestions, we end up in one of those family pubs that aren't really pubs. I can't complain, she has to think of the two boys after all. They wouldn't feel comfortable in the Red Lion, and the Red Lion wouldn't feel comfortable with them, for a few years yet. This is really going to restrict my drinking choices today though.

So me and Dad have arranged to meet at the bus-stop near his place. Dad doesn't like to drive much anymore and I'm not planning on being the designated driver today. That's no problem. You can go to a lot of places on public transport, more than you might think, if you are prepared to do the appropriate research. Fortunately, today we just need one bus and a bit of a walk, and it's a nice day. Dad has his bus pass. I have a pocketful of change, mostly procured from the Red Lion throughout the week.

"Happy Birthday, Dad!" I shout as I approach the bus stop. He waves back to me but opts not to say anything until I get near enough to talk normally. "Thanks, son. Another one already, eh? Are *you* looking forward to this?"
"Of course, of course. It's your birthday!" I exclaim enthusiastically.
"Yes, but this is not your usual sort of place is it? Nor mine."
"Yeah, well there may be one pint I can stomach if I'm lucky. There's always a Guinness to fall back on."
Dad sighs. "I was referring to all the kids we'll be sharing the room with. It's no secret that you are not a natural with the smaller humans."
"Hmm, that's not fair...ok it is fair, but you know, it is hard to know what to say to them. It's been too long since I've been one. There are so few common frames of reference."

"There must be thousands…" Dad starts.
"*Interesting* common frames of reference," I specify. "For example, I have no interest in the Top 40."
"I used to say the very same to you."
"Yeah Dad, but you couldn't keep away, could you? You still used to stay at the door watching Top of the Pops, and tutting once in a while, so you must have had some interest, despite what you said. I don't even have the energy to find out what to tut about nowadays."
"Don't forget, I even took you to see your first gig when you were a teenager. I didn't have to do that."
"Oh yeah, sorry about that. If it helps, I don't listen to them much anymore myself."
"You don't say, Dan. Me neither."
"Yeah, but it was still a good night. My first gig! You never forget that."
"I shall never forget that night, no." Dad shakes his head sadly.
"Don't be so sarcastic. Well, *I* was glad you were there anyway. You weren't even that embarrassing."
"Thanks a lot, son. Anyway, I was glad to be there for you. Well, further back at the bar anyway. No, you're right, it was a good night. I'll always remember your face, full to the brim with excitement and wonder."
"Ok, ok, less of that. The band really wasn't *that* good. In hindsight anyway. But imagine going to Tom and Ethan's first gig now? That would most likely be seriously dreadful."
"Well, try and be nice to your nephews today at least."
"I will Dad, but they may not notice. You know, while on the subject, someone down the pub did accuse me of being immature recently."
"Really?"
"Really. But if I'm so immature then how come I don't relate to kids at all then?"

"That, Dan, would need some more research. Why don't you do some when you grow up?"
He's just playing with me. I pretend to be in a huff as the bus pulls up, but that doesn't stop him smiling to himself. We get on the bus, then, of course, head straight upstairs to the front seat.

Rachel, Tom, Ethan, and Rachel's husband, Don are already there at our table when we arrive, sipping on wine and soft drinks respectively. Don is having a zero percent lager. Don't get me started on that. Don, by the way, is also the father of the boys, in case you're concerned about that sort of thing. We get on fine, me and Don, but don't see each other out of context. Me and Dad are feeling ready for a drink after our walk and I check out the pumps on the bar on my way past. I think they actually have a real beer. I've never heard of it but I shall try it anyway. After we say our hellos and happy birthdays I order one of those. Dad, to my surprise, just asks for a bitter shandy. He knows this will cause a reaction from myself so just shrugs and says, "I just fancy one. It *is* my birthday."
"Exactly," I say, which could easily mean two opposite things.

During my second pint, to prove my maturity, or otherwise – I have now confused myself on this matter – I attempt to engage with the nephews. I naively expected that this would get easier as they got older but the teenage years have proved the most difficult yet. I don't know why. I was a perfectly pleasant teenager. They are both currently highly engaged with their phones so I decide to try this line:
"Hey, what phone have you got there? I've got a…"
I have to pull mine out to check the model number of the phone I have. It's seldom on my mind. They look at my phone with mild disapproval and some disinterest, then

show me theirs. They have the same one. They look nice. Nicer than mine anyway. You can tell their phones apart because each one has a different cover, representing a different football team. Or it might be rugby. I elect not to tread on that uncertain territory. It never even occurred to me to have a cover on my phone, never mind what I might choose to have on it if I did have one.

"Nice," is all I manage to say. Ethan's phone vibrates in my hand. He grabs it back and mumbles "Gotta check this." And that is that.

Rachel is chatting away at Dad, so I turn to Don for comfort. This is normally a decent option but I'm nearly at the end of my second pint, with a third one on the way, and he's not drinking. The uneven nature of these situations always makes me feel uncomfortable. When everyone is equally drunk even the stupid stuff you say sounds sensible to all present. But the sober person will see all the dumb things said for what they actually are. I steel myself to try and feel sober again. I don't know why. It didn't work when I sneaked home with Mum waiting up and it won't work now.

"You doing alright, Don?"

"Yeah, not bad, not bad."

"Designated driver today, I see."

"Yep, my turn. Don't worry, I'll be cashing this one in next weekend."

Hmm, small talk done. Nothing else to go on yet. He's waiting for me to say something. I say something.

"Business ok then?" Don is some kind of equity partner in some kind of engineering firm. I'm a little hazy on the details, but the question should be safe enough. Come on, Don, give me something here.

"Well, there are difficult market conditions out there at the moment, but we have some good long term contracts and they are seeing us through. Looks like we are going to have a good year after all, once the next quarterlies come through."

"Glad to hear it." I say. We're quickly on small talk auto-pilot now. I ask him for more details, mainly so he doesn't ask me about my work. He's happy to provide me with all sorts of details, until the conversation inevitably fades and I excuse myself away to the Gents.

I'm conscious that I haven't spoken much to Rachel, who I happen to get on perfectly well with since we both left home, and I catch her at the bar on my way back.
"Hey, sis. How's the wine?"
"Fine. I have way better back home, but what can you do."
"Dad seems on decent form today, yeah?"
"I think so. Has he mentioned, you know, *Mum*, much today?" she asks me.
"No, not at all. I think that's off the table."
"Good, we should just try and have a nice day today."
"Indeed. Hey, not seen you for ages. How are things?" I ask her.
"That lot," she nods over to our table, "keep me on my toes. It's enough to turn you to drink!"
"I thought all that would be getting easier by now. Aren't the boys all self-sufficient yet?" She gives me a look. I continue digging that hole regardless. "You know, aren't they a wiz in the kitchen or a dab hand with the hoover?"
"What planet are you on, Daniel?" she says. "They're getting lazier by the day, I swear. All of them!"
"Oh, sorry…"
"I think you forget what *you* were like at that age. It was all books and no housework as far as I can recall."
"Ah, well maybe…"
"Don's being a pain in the arse as well. I know something is going on at work…"

"You mean, like, *something*?" I try and raise my eyebrows and look concerned at the same time. I don't think this works for the observer, but it makes sense in my brain at least.

"No, not that something! At least I wasn't thinking that until now, thank you very much! No, he's been working late and getting stressed and the like. I've overheard some heated phone conversations with Eric…"

"Er, Eric?"

"His partner. His *business* partner, Dan. Pay attention, will you? No, I think they might be in a bit of trouble. He won't say anything though. He doesn't talk to me about any of this."

"He just said to me that they were doing alright. Good, even."

"Well, he would wouldn't he? He wants everything to look normal. He wants us to look normal."

We look over at the four of them sitting at the table, drinking, eating, chatting, texting, having a pretty good time in their own different ways. We take a sip of our drinks and pause for a moment. Rachel then waves her hand around the room, across all the diners before us.

"*Everyone* looks normal from back here, don't they?"

I look. "They do, Rach. They sure do."

Someone (Rachel) must have let slip that there is a birthday at our table. The music suddenly is turned up and 'Happy Birthday to you' blares over the tannoy. Then, as if from nowhere, a cake with a balloon hanging off it and a candle on top that looks like a sparkler, arrives at our table. A few people at tables near us clap and smile. They probably think this is all for one of the boys. I think the birthday surprise package here must just be 'one-size-fits-all'. That is, for all ages. Dad looks equally pleased and embarrassed when the cake is placed in front of him. The clapping then fades abruptly at that point. Rachel gets her phone out and starts to wave us into a shot for her camera.

"Move in, move in a bit. Tom? That's fine. Dan. Dan! Get into shot, you idiot!"

I resist a while but then join the group for the shot. Then the waiter swiftly offers to take a picture so Rachel can get into shot too. All part of the service, no doubt. She doesn't need asking twice.

I remember a song I heard a while back, advising you to get a picture of people you love while you can, since they may not all be there next time. I remember reflecting when I first heard it just how true that was. Two years ago to this very day we never bothered getting a shot of us all while Mum was still here. That would have been a nice picture to have now. But we never took the opportunity then, and the opportunity never came back, so the picture never existed.

Say cheese.

FIG.2

fig.2 The electron travels towards the screen where it will pass through one of the two slits

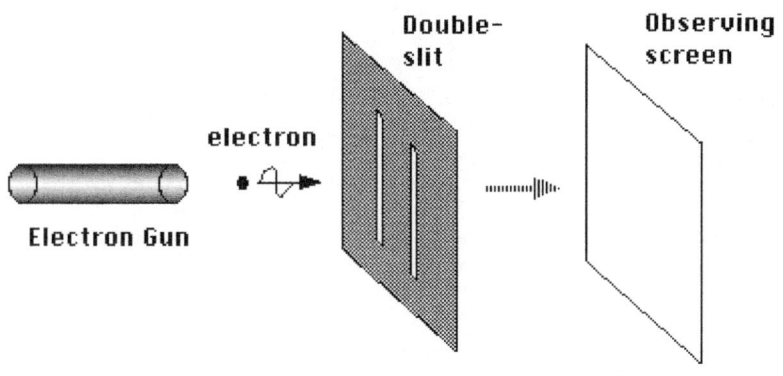

"Say cheese," was also what I had ended up saying to Jess and Adam, while I was still sitting with them in the pub. There was no need really, they were already smiling from ear to ear, both well-practiced in the art of the couple-shot. Still, it's nice to say something like that isn't it?

As I am walking down the street towards Dad's house, I think about the picture that I had just taken. Through the lens, Jess and Adam looked so invincible together, like nothing could ever touch them. Like no impending tragedy could ever puncture through the emotional armour they had created for themselves. I must have photos like that, photos of me and Jen, now hidden away somewhere. I know that those moments don't last.

Oh no. There's the house already.

Chapter 3

Me and my sister don't argue as much as she would like. Conflict averse she called me. I didn't want to argue.

Chapter 4

Say, have you ever seen a Yorkshire terrier try and intimidate a police horse? No, not imitate. *Intimidate*. Anyway, I have. Just now, on my way to the pub. That's *to* the pub, not on my way back, you understand. This wasn't a drunken hallucination thing. It was intrinsically funny, as you may imagine, that little thing yapping away at the giant in front of it. The horse (and the copper) were most patient. The dog owner was a bit ineffectual though. Waddling after her dog, waving at it like she was swatting flies and calling out instructions like 'come here' and 'here boy' in such a tone that, unless you spoke English, probably sounded like 'Good boy' or 'Carry on harassing that horse'. I just sat on the bench and smirked to myself, catching the odd glance of strangers, who were equally amused. We were all briefly joined at that moment, just by merely sharing that inconsequential experience. Maybe there's some deep metaphor in there somewhere, which will tell me something deep about my life. But I can't be bothered to find it. Neither should you. It would only be coincidence after all, surely. Back down the Red Lion I couldn't help but notice some guy who was sitting at the bar, particularly enjoying the first sip of his pint, just as I'm getting my first drink in. He's drinking a pint of Summer Hummer, my current favourite. I catch his eye as I look over.

"I've been in Bruges for two weeks," he says, as if by way of explanation. I nod, take my change and my pint, but stay at the bar.
"Never been," I say. "Was it nice?"
"The place is beautiful. Pretty chilled out too. There's worse places to get sent to for work."
"Right, right. Aren't they famous for their beer over there

then?"
"Yeah, they are. That's the thing really."
"What, no good?"
"No, it was good. But it's just so strong. I made a few, er, miscalculations before I got used to it."
"Ha, those trappist beers can be dangerous, right?"
"Those I knew about. Steered clear. But everything is dangerous over there. Your standard pint is at least 6%."
"Ouch."
"Then it just goes up from there. I had this brown ale. Just a small one. Then when I stood up my head was all spinning. I'd only had two."
"Hmm, yes you would not normally expect two to do that."
"Worst thing was that the toilets were up this long spiral staircase."
"Bad combination."
"You're not wrong. I was hanging on with both hands, taking one step at a time, like some five year old. All the way up and all the way down. Had to make sure we were somewhere else before the next bladder call, you know, with more convenient facilities."
"Don't you get these beer menus where you can check the, er, potency then?"
"Yeah, you can, you can. Not everywhere though. Anyway, it's impossible to get a safe pint, like this one, over there. A fruit beer maybe. But some of those can be a bit mad."
I look over at the pump where Summer Hummer is sitting. 3.8% says the sign on the pump. You can sure drink a few of those before you get staircase issues.
"Trouble is," he continues, "I'm trained to drink at a certain pace, to take a swig at a certain angle. I'm trained to around 4% in my glass. If I go off piste it gets messy pretty quickly."
I laugh, although by his face I don't think he meant the pun.
"Yeah, me too," I say. "I like a session so I keep to the

session beers. But you know, it's us that are different. The Brits. Most countries have beer, or lager really, that is stronger than most of our pints. A Belgian would probably spend a night here wondering why he could still find where the door was at the end of the evening." I'm off on a roll now, on one of my favourite subjects. He seems happy to listen. "It's all to do with taxes."
"Taxes?"
"Yeah. Centuries ago taxes were put on beer depending on the strength. The weaker the beer, the less it cost. A pint of the Trappist…"
"Ooh, no. You wouldn't buy a pint of that."
"Hmm, well a pint of that would be inordinately expensive, as well as ill-advised, so people here got used to drinking the weaker stuff."
"Those European governments missed out on plenty of good taxes in that case."
"I'm sure they found other ways. Anyway, so with that and grain shortages in the wars and all that, we all got used to drinking this sort of thing." I hold up my pint.
"Right."
"Thing is, I love it. You can try loads of them, all the different flavours, and keep your head on. Well, for a little longer anyway. And, importantly, you can have a *pint*."
"Yeah, those little bottles and glasses seemed a bit wrong. They were right, Jesus they were the right size in the circumstances, but they just felt wrong in your hand. Too small, you know."
"Yeah, I know. Ha, the worst thing my mother ever said to me was that a pint glass looked too big in my hands, and I should drinks halves."
"How rude," he laughs.
"Yeah, that was one bit of maternal advice I did not take. The pint is just the perfect size right? Big enough to enjoy the experience, small enough to try a few different ones." I

hold my glass up so the remaining sun of the day, filtering through the pub window, filters further through the beer.
"Beautiful."
"You really do like your beer, don't you mate?" he says, as he looks over to grab the attention of the landlord.
And so on.
I do have friends by the way. Actual friends. It's not all talking to strangers. Me and Jez, plus Amy, who you already know, were out tonight for example. Because it was Band Night. We didn't know any of the bands but that doesn't matter. Not at all. Familiarity is not the point. There is just something so life affirming about hearing anything live, right there in front of your face, regardless of the genre or even the quality. We saw the poster on the way in. I mean, really, lack of familiarity was indeed guaranteed tonight. Where do they get these acts from? The poster said this:

Red Lion Music Night.
Playing tonight:
Gladstone English
Tantric Love Rabbit
Evostick Flashback

Sounds good.

There's not much chat of course during the early proceedings when the bands are on. Just the odd staccato sentence yelled into the adjacent earhole. Not really for conveying information as such, but rather just to confirm the connection between us. So nothing new learned this evening as yet. Later in the toilets, however, I overhear this illuminating observation from some local wag:
"You know how it is. Drink ten pints. Pass fifteen. And still put on weight!"
True, I expect. More research required here too.

"If you're in, urine," says Jez, again, and heads off to the Gents himself. While he tends to his requirements Amy asks of me, "How are you mate? Been a while. Found anyone special yet?"
"Well, I've ruled out a couple." I say.
"*You* ruled them out?"
"Well, they were kind enough to give me a little help."
"It's nice to be helpful."
"And you?" Since I wasn't specific, you may have assumed that Jez and Amy were an item. If you actually meet them you may very well think that too. However, they are not.
"I'm done with that." Takes a sip of cider.
"You can't mean that."
She raises her eyes over the lip of her glass in mid sip, and stares me down until I take it back.
"Alright, you can mean that," I say to appease her wrath.
Jez comes back and leans in. "Check *her* out over there mate."
"Who are you talking to?" I ask.
"You, you turnip. Her. Pink streak, Flowing skirts. Just your type."
"Nah, you're all right mate. Don't feel like it. Go for it yourself if you like."
"What's wrong with her, man? She looks lovely enough to me." I can't help but notice he's still standing here though.
Amy looks over and peruses for a moment, while I concentrate firmly on my pint.
"Nice," she says. "Does she perhaps look a little too 'helpful' to you Dan?"
I stare over the lip of my pint at her. This has no effect at all on Amy. She turns to Jez.
"She looks a little too helpful."
Jez has no idea what that means, presumably, but he doesn't skip a beat.
"Darn. Did I get that wrong then. So much for first

impressions, eh? Right, we are definitely going to need another round before Tantric Love Rabbit."
"Yay!" That was me.
"It's your round." Amy assures me.
"I knew that."
I did know that too.

No word of a lie. We have all just danced to 'New York New York'. Gladstone English do a much better version of this than the name may suggest. If the name suggests anything to you at all. This night is getting nicely out of hand. Just wait until the karaoke starts. I have lined up 'Through the Barricades' or perhaps 'Love on the Rocks'. Not because I'm feeling lovelorn or nothing. Or no more than usual at any rate, given the stage of the evening. It's just that I can just about get away with these two tunes somehow. One time, I got approached by a Glaswegian fella after singing 'Love on the Rocks' in a strange pub on New Year's Eve. You know, one of those places that you would never dream of going into if it wasn't a special night or something. Anyway, I gave a particularly impassioned performance this time. I always do now, after this one very drunk guy way back had pumped his fist at me during a lacklustre rendition of the first chorus. Not in a threatening way, not at all, just to encourage me a little more towards Neil Diamond's level of emotional engagement. Duly chastised, I went for it by chorus two and was rewarded by a big thumbs up as he staggered back across the front of the stage. So anyway, now back at this New Year I had just finished 'Love on the Rocks'. I had done a decent job I thought, and was emoting back down to normal level when I heard:
"Hey pal!"
The accent was unmistakable. I was quickly back down to earth with a bump, heart a-pounding.

"Hey pal!"
"Er, yes?"
"You spoke to me pal…"
"No, I…"
"You spoke to me there. From the heart. I'm gonna buy you a drink. Don't you go sayin' no now!"
"Wouldn't dream of it," I assured him.
"Yer cannot get Glava here, which that singin' would've deserved. No decent whisky in this pub. But name yer tipple. Go on."
In my distinct relief as to the way this was now going, I somehow plumped for a tequila. The story stops dead right there, I'm afraid, for fairly obvious reasons.

And so the three of us now sit slumped in our seats, back at our table, slightly sweaty but happy. Someone says:
"You are my true friends you know. And you know what true friends are, right? Your true friends, your *true* friends, are those who will lay down their dignity for the joy of the moment."
"Yay!" said someone else.
Pregnant pause, "And expect the same back."
"Yay!"
"Jeez Jez, that's a bit deep."
Pause.
"How much have we had?"
About the right amount, I think.

We meet up again on Sunday, for afternoon drinks, as tradition dictates. That way you can numb yourself to the week ahead without doing too much damage to your poor future Monday self, provided you can stop in time of course. Sunday drinking is like a decompression chamber, coming up after the weekend's main events. There will come a point, say around six o'clock where maybe one of you, and common sense, dictate that *that* should indeed be that, and you should all go home. But, as often will happen, one of you might not be quite ready. Maybe they are a bit worried about some meeting or deadline or other at work, and need 'just one more'.

"Just one more," Amy says, "I've got my end of probation interview tomorrow and it's stressing me out just thinking about it."
"I thought you didn't even like your job," Jez observes.
"Yes, but I want them to like *me*."
"Hmm, I see. Ok then." he swiftly concedes.
"Fine, one more, but let's try a change of scene," I suggest. "One at the Shakespeare so we don't get too comfortable. I can't afford to be too wasted tomorrow."
"Deal."
"Deal."
The Shakespeare, you see, is ok for Sunday lunch and a bit beyond, but gets a little scuzzy later on in the evening as the serious drinkers, even by our standards, take over. We won't want to be there beyond eight o'clock so even if 'one' becomes 'two' we should still be able to rein ourselves in. Trust me, this is my area of expertise.

Between the Red Lion and the Shakespeare is our old junior school. Mine and Amy's anyway. It's been a while since we've been this way, so we stop off for a moment. Jez peers over the wall to look at the old playground.
"So little versions of you two used to run around *here* then?" Jez asks, sounding a little disappointed.
"This was the boy's yard so mainly me, yeah." I pause to look around too. "It wasn't a car park then of course. That's new."
"Hmm, yes," adds Amy, "that does sour the memory somewhat. I seem to remember cornering you for a kiss somewhere around bay five or bay six…"
"Is that a euphemism?" Jez lofts in.

"…And I got away!" I declare, punching the air. Then I immediately get a little deflated. "What was all that about? Running away from girls actually willing to kiss me? Life can have cruel timing. Man, this place looks so small now. Even taking into account the parking spaces. I thought that the headlong run into the brick wall at the bottom over there was *much* longer than that. In my mind's eye, the recollection of that run, or better still, sliding along in the winter, is of sheer death-defying feats and terrifying speeds. It looks pretty low-key from here."
"Where do the kids play now then, I wonder," wonders Amy, then "…hey, what do you mean 'got away'? Since when were you ever quicker than me anyway? If I had wanted to catch you, Daniel, you'd have been caught." Amy insists.
"You two are weird," concludes Jez, and rightly so. "Right, about time for that pint then."

Nothing stays the same, no matter how much we try to resist the changes. But *we* don't stay the same ourselves, so how can we expect anything else to? Ah well, The Shakespeare calls. We had two in the end, thought about a third, relented, then went home and went to bed. And then the week began.

Chapter 5

So today I've been chatting with Dad again. Not down the pub. That's never seems to happen for some reason, not these days anyway. We were back at my old house, where I grew up. It looks just the same as ever but smaller of course, like the old school playground. I have no idea how I used to fit so comfortably into my old bedroom. I can hardly turn around in it now. Despite this though, the house feels ever so empty without Mum. I don't know how Dad stays here. I really don't.

On my way there I have to cross this bypass and wait for the lights. Sometimes, when I remember, I look at the faces of the people in their cars as they pass by and count the happy faces. It's quite safe. No one ever looks back. I press the button on the pelican crossing.
"Wait," says the sign. I wait.
None.
None.
One. Good start.
Still one.
Tum de dum.
Still one.
Blimey, still one. Cheer up folks.
Singing to herself. That counts. Two.
Lights turn to amber. No point checking the car that slows down. That driver will always be miserable. Like they've been punched in the guts or something. This one here will be catching up to the back end of the driving diva within two minutes, but that apparently doesn't prevent the crashing sense that the universe is against you at that moment, when the lights turn red on you. Two. Not bad, I

think, as I cross the road and head down to my Dad's street, proceeding to whistle something tuneless.

Dad looked out of sorts when he opened the door, but he's not one to fuss and neither am I, so I breezed in and blithely headed to the kettle as usual, patting him on the shoulder as I passed by. Once we sit down I can tell by the look on his face he is missing Mum again. It is Mother's Day after all. The only question is whether he is going to admit it or not. Dad is not one for over-emoting, but from time to time the situation can overcome him.

I could tell you a bit about my Mum I suppose. She was a very mothering Mum, like she was born to the role, although I expect most children mistakenly think that of their parents. Like their Mum and Dad never had to learn to grow up themselves, get scared, or have dreams of their own. And then all the compromises and the dreams get packed away. Forgotten or replaced. Anyway, she was particularly mothering to me, more so than to Rachel, says Rachel. I remember that she liked dressing me when I was pretty sure I could manage a decent job of it myself. But I didn't mind. It was nice to be looked after. I could do with some looking after now. Not that, I can dress myself now, but you know what I mean. I miss her.

As for the relationship between her and Dad, it was hard to tell. They did not readily express any emotion in front of me and my sister, but, despite this, I know now just how much Dad loved her. All the barriers came crashing down at the funeral, you see. All that grief and sadness. All that relief and exhaustion. You have to go for it at funerals though, I have learned. That's probably why we have them, right across this planet, from culture to culture. If you don't, all those emotions just get bottled up inside and start to fester. Dad had no intention of letting his emotions go that day, I reckon. But by the end of proceedings it was like his heart and his soul, and a good deal of his dignity, had been cruelly splattered all over the pub where we held the post-funeral party. Nothing too dramatic, he just kept breaking down in tears in mid-conversation. He was just trying to be too strong, but he had so little strength left by then that he just kept breaking down with no warning to whoever he happened to be with. Me, the funeral director, the landlord, the landlord's dog. In due course he would gather himself together, but only to begin the cycle again. Later, he was mortified at the scene he imagined that he had created. Not one person minded though. Why would you? It's a healthy and natural reaction in my book. I'm pretty sure that the dog didn't mind either.

Soon after that I came back to live here. That was fine. London's scales had well and truly tipped against me by then anyway, Jen being gone and all, so it just seemed like the right thing to do. It was the easy thing to do at least.

By the time I was all grown up Mum would always call me on the morning of my birthday, at 10.25 am, or I would call her. That was the time of my birth, there or thereabouts. She usually had to call me, as by the time I was eighteen I was invariably somewhere else in the country, happily being distracted, in London with Jen, my girlfriend, or visiting mates. She would always start by saying "Happy Birthday mate" for some long-lost reason. I would then say "…and thank you for giving birth!" This amused her, and didn't embarrass me too much so I was happy to. A small tradition of sorts for what it's worth. A connection.

It was hard on Dad the way she went, though. But he never talked about it too much and today he says nothing about Mum at all. He has taken to telling me more stories from his past of late for some reason. Today he tells me again about factory life in the '70s. It sounded mostly horrendous to me, but I expect it wasn't so bad, not like being down the mines or being in the war. He tells me about lunchtime at the factory, which is one of my favourites, so always worth another listen.

Early 70's back up North, where Dad comes from, is like a different world to me. Not quite in black and white in my mind, but in that grainy, washed-out colour instead that doesn't quite seem in focus. I tell Dad this, but suffix this thought by saying that it probably was just as colourful then in real life as it is now. He says no, he remembers it as being pretty drab in real life too. Despite being a voracious reader now he wasn't one for school much in his youth. So he had done as little learning as possible there and just breezed into the nearest factory, the same everyone else did. There you had machines as big as rooms, drilling or cutting massive bits of steel, but to a mind-bogglingly tiny accuracy, or 'tolerance' as they called it. In amongst all this were the workers, almost hidden, seemingly almost irrelevant to the proceedings, just another part of the machine, as the noise clattered through the air all day without respite. This is my imagination off again, by the way. Dad does not describe it in these terms.

"The air smelled, no, *tasted* of metal," is what he actually says, "and bloody deafening it was. But you got used to it all after a time. You had to work piecework mostly so you just got your head down and worked with the machines and the conveyor belts until you felt part of them. Never clock watched, you couldn't take your eye off what you were doing. You just wouldn't earn enough otherwise."
My work spreadsheets were not so high-maintenance. I shall look at them in a different light from now on. I imagine a cell on the spreadsheet opening up and telling me to stop daydreaming and get back to work. Ha.

"But eventually, and often to my surprise, came the lunchtime siren," Dad continues, "so we stopped whatever we were doing and headed off."

"To the canteen?" I ask, knowing this is not the case. This story has often been told in our family but is always worth another spin, as if it were the first time recounted. Everyone always played their part. Revered story-teller. Fascinated audience. And Jasper played the semi-interested cat, when he was with us.

"No. Not to the canteen. To the pub! And there they were. Dozens of pints of Scotch all lined up the full length of the bar, waiting for us. Not whiskey mind but our Scotch, like a dark bitter, you know."

"Mmm." I affirm. First time I heard this tale I had no idea at all. I could easily bore you for an hour on this very subject these days.

"What they did, the barmaids, was fill up each glass with a half before the siren even went off. Then as soon as it did they rushed to fill up all the glasses to the top with the other half. There was no hand pull back then you know, just a button that dispensed half a pint at a time. That's' why we need the bigger pint glasses, to fit in all the head."

"Mmm." I love those big pint glasses. Can't get them down here.

"They did this because there was just no way that they could serve us all in time if they pulled all the pints when we got there. But they knew we were all coming so knew how many to get ready. They made it work. We all descended on the place in one go, you see. We had to just rush in, drink our pint, rush back and get back to work."

"Did it ever occur to you that you didn't have to go to the pub every lunchtime?" I ask, rhetorically, "or whether it was such a good idea to operate heavy machinery when nicely topped up with booze?"

He just laughs and shrugs. "Seems mad now. Made sense

then. That's all I can say. Got rid of the taste of metal at the time though. Strange, but now I swear I can taste the metal whenever I go back up there and have a Scotch."
I remind myself to also be thankful that my Golden Ale does not taste of Excel.

In return I tell Dad of the Six o'clock Swill, a bizarre phenomenon that occurred in Australia and New Zealand. I had recently seen a programme about it, and had followed up with a bit of reading. I think it started during the First World War but despite being a monumentally bad idea, lasted up until the sixties. So this, along with Franco, and Love Thy Neighbour and other things, are a collection of events that for me feel like ancient history, but were almost within my own lifetime! Anyway, the Six o'clock Swill was born out of a temperance movement, which were commonplace during the war, since everyone had to work at winning rather than getting bladdered. I kind of get that in principle but I wasn't there so I won't judge. Anyway, some bright spark in Australia reckons that if they close the pubs down at six, thus giving the workers only one hour to drink after work, then problems with drinking and hangovers and lost production and so on would all be solved in one go.

"Sounds fair enough, eh Dad?" I say, to make sure he's still listening.
"If you insist. Not much fun though."
"Well, it didn't turn out as expected. What actually happened was that everyone rushed down to the pub dead on five and drank as much as was humanly possible in the hour they had. Come six o'clock they were all chucked out onto the streets, twatted to high heaven, with nothing better to do than fight. It was a mess. But no one changed the law. For decades!"
"Jesus, how did they ever manage to get that arseholed in

an hour?" asks Dad, reasonably.

"Well, the Aussie landlords weren't going to miss out were they? They were still going to get their evening's takings in no matter what. So they stripped out all the seats and carpets and the pumps. In came easy to wash down tiles and standing-only areas…"

"Well you don't strictly need a seat if you're not stopping."

"…Indeed, standing-only areas and what I can only describe as a hosepipe for dispensing the beer. It's true, I saw some old footage of this on the TV. These places were joyless. The landlord would just keep the hosepipe running and filled up any glass that came near it. Meanwhile the floor, and the punters, and anything else near the nozzle were just getting covered in beer."

"Makes my lunchtimes seem positively civilised," Dad observes.

"You're not wrong. You know what your clothes smell like when someone's spilled their beer on you? The whole country must have smelled like that, ALL the time!" I'm getting a bit animated, not sure why. It's not like I shall ever have to suffer this fate. Perhaps I am too empathetic sometimes. I should work on that.

"So that little plan backfired then." Dad says. "That would have happened here too I expect. The eleven o'clock swill was bad enough."

"Too right. So, rather than stopping people drinking it just made them drink faster. Much faster in this case. Took all the fun out of it, but they still did it. Oh well, such is human nature, when you think about it."

"A sobering thought." Dad jests. At least I think he's joking. He plays that particular one dead straight.

This is all very nice but throughout the proceedings Dad keeps looking at this piece of paper as if it were a list of an actor's prompt lines or something. He doesn't let me see what is on it, which is slightly off-putting, and he looks a little flustered when I try. No matter, after an hour or so I have to get off down to the pub anyway.

Like I said, it was Mother's Day, which is why Mum has been on my mind a little more than usual I suppose. I *know* these special days are supposed to be there for positive reasons, like Father's Day, anniversaries, even Valentine's Day for God's sake. But remember that for many people, these events just dig up old wounds, to mix my metaphors. Not to mention all these other 'special' days that are just increasingly becoming one big marketing tool after another to shift a load of tat you don't really need. What's wrong with just saying to someone that you love them? That costs nothing. But why isn't that good enough anymore? Ha, I'm being a little facetious of course because saying 'I love you' is something my family were never very good at, and consequently I never have been either. But we seem to have managed without the words and we somehow know how we feel about each other without them. This is possibly a bit of an English affliction, but does a card, or balloon or even flowers really fill that gap? For some maybe, but I don't think so myself. This conversation often comes up between me and Jez and Amy so we have together formed the 'No Tat Alliance' for such occasions.

Therefore, today we are in the midst of what may become a bit of a tradition. Instead of cards and flowers etc. we all agreed that we would bring our mothers to the pub instead on Mother's Day. For lunch, and maybe a drink or two, you never know. Spending time rather than money. I can't join in properly of course, since Mum is no longer with us, but that's fine. When we first decided to do this last year we talked it all out and I drunkenly insisted to Jez and Amy that this was a still good idea and I would still like to be part of it. Unusually, when we sobered up it still seemed like a good idea so we did do it and we all had a nice afternoon. We talked about Mum from time to time that day. It was emotional but felt good in a way. So we agreed we would do it again.

I arrived first, naturally. I normally like to get one in before anyone else arrives. Get myself settled. Most people don't like being the first to arrive. In some groups everyone turns up at least half an hour late just to make sure they are not there first, which is just crazy if you think about it. I feel that not being first is a missed opportunity myself. Looking around, there were no families here - this pub is more famed for its beer than its food - and I would imagine that most people would now be starting to populate the myriad restaurants up and down the High Street, rather than coming in here. The 'No Tat Alliance' likes to do things differently though, and display a bit of loyalty. Rachel, by the way, will be at home, suffering the approximations of cooking courtesy of Don and the two boys, on her own Mother's Day. I try not to think what Dad is up to now. I offered but he didn't want to come.

Amy arrives first with her Mum. Betty is her name. They are very alike, these two, almost like sisters. In fact, out of the two of them I find Amy to be the bossiest, but maybe that's because Betty doesn't get enough opportunity to boss me around. She probably would take up that opportunity if it came along, I suspect. A lot of people do. I set myself up for it, I know. I kiss them both on the cheek, just the one, I'm not European after all, and they sit down. As Amy goes to the bar, me and Betty exchange some pleasantries.
"How are you keeping, Betty?"
"Fine, Dan, fine. And you?"
"Tip top, top top."
Once that's all over with we can actually get on with a proper conversation. I've known Betty most of my life,

since before I started school in fact. Amy was in my class. Myself and Betty were never close as such – I was a boy after all and so was not part of Amy's inner circle for some years - but I always thought she looked quite fun. A cool Mum. I was right as it turned out.

"Just been to Zumba this morning. Thought I would get up early and squeeze a session in before hitting the wine here. It makes you feel so so good, you know." This is Betty speaking, you will have guessed. *I* don't know how it makes you feel, and never will. I could be polite but I decide to tell her just that. She normally likes me to be a bit cheeky.

"No, I don't know it makes you feel, Betty, as you very well know. And I never shall. Leotards just don't seem to suit me. And neither does being vertical on a Sunday morning."

"Oh, I know what you mean Daniel. I used to like nothing better than being horizontal on a Sunday morning myself. Chance would be a fine thing now! Zumba will have to do instead." She laughs loudly. I pretend to choke on my pint, which makes her laugh even more. Amy turns back towards us from the bar, grinning. I just raise my eyebrows and shrug my shoulders.

"I don't know what you mean," I say, knowing entirely what she means. Thankfully, Jez and his Mum choose this moment to arrive. Her name is Chloe. Amy looks over and groans, raising her hands to the air in mock indignation. By a matter of seconds she has just copped for a big round. Jez raises his thumbs up and shouts over "Whatever we're having today, plus a G&T! Cheers Ames." More kissing and introductory pleasantries ensue, as you would expect, and we settle down for the afternoon.

Betty and Chloe know each other reasonably well, as it goes. Not from Zumba. That's not Chloe's thing at all. But

from when they were at school themselves. They were not in the same year though. Betty, it transpires, was in the same class as Chloe's older brother, Edward, and as we are now gathering, fancied him a bit back then.
"How is your Edward these days, Clo?" Betty asks. "Still asks after me, does he?"
"Not since the seventies, no, Bet. I'll tell him you were asking after him though."
They both laugh. "You will do no such thing. He missed his chance on the trip to Scarborough."
And so on. My drinking pace has upped somewhat. I blame the way the conversation has turned since the other humans joined my afternoon. I could never imagine my parents talking like that. It bothers Amy and Jez not a jot however, and they are both rather enjoying showing off their Mums to today's patrons of the Red Lion, waving across the bar from time to time at the familiar faces. Time drifts by effortlessly, and we are all getting on ever so well, like a bunch of friends really.

I met Jez when we were a little older, in sixth form, so I didn't know Chloe quite as well as Betty. By then, all parents were terribly embarrassing and you always had to extricate yourselves from their presence as soon as possible. She always seemed nice enough though, and it only takes a couple of gin and tonics for her to relax into the group. Jez gets his laid back nature from his Dad, clearly. I'm having a good time, I really am, but it's hard to ignore the asymmetry at play here.

Presently it's Jez's turn for a round, and after a short while he comes back with a tray. This is usually frowned upon and seen as cheating, but in current company we shall let that go. He passes the drinks around. There are six. A sherry sits at the side of the table, next to me, but without an owner.

"Here's to Di. Bottoms up," he says. He can be really thoughtful sometimes, can Jez. The time has come. We raise our glasses. Variously, we all say:
"To Di."
"Cheers Di."
"Bless you, Di.
"Bottoms up!"
"Hi Mum."
And we take a drink. It doesn't count if you don't take a drink. I stare at the sherry for a while. I don't normally drink sherry, who does, but it reminds me of Christmas, and of Mum, so it's the right choice. Everyone stays silent for a moment and the background buzz of the pub begins to pervade our little bubble.
"Cheers. Thanks Mum. Thanks for being my Mum." I say, and neck the sherry down in one. This didn't happen last year, but I sense this is how traditions are born.

I pop into Dad's again on the way home. It's not strictly on the way home, but I've had a good afternoon, I'm in a buoyant mood, and the others are going back to see their Dads anyway, to return their maternal progenitors, and report on proceedings. I did phone ahead a pint or two ago but Dad is asleep when I knock on the door. After the third knock, he gets to the door, a little groggy looking. He wordlessly turns back down the hallway to let me in.

Once I've made a cuppa for the both us, I tell him about my afternoon. He takes all this in quietly. He vaguely knows Chloe so asks after her. I say she is fine. I think about it, then I tell him about the sherry.
"Did she like the sherry?" he asks? "Your Mam is very particular about that you know."
"Yeah, Dad. I'm sure she would have liked it." I humour his use of the present tense, although I do find this odd, as he has never been one to use the afterlife as a crutch before,

not even at the funeral.
"Good, good."
"Yeah, it was nice. Felt like the right thing to do."
"So, did she not come back with you then?"

It's at this point that I finally managed to read the piece of paper he was carrying with him. He had placed it on the table and had still been looking at it occasionally. It had been bugging me again somewhat but not enough to mention it. It said this:
"You know this one. This is your son".

Oh.

All those little clues I had been ignoring for such a while now suddenly coalesced into a single thought. Calling Rachel 'Diane' for example, or forgetting to meet me occasionally and pretending he hadn't when I knocked on the door. So many more, now I think about it. Oh no, now *this* is happening. *Dad is not well.*

Broke my heart a little, that, I don't mind saying. And it was a turning point if ever there was one.

CHAPTER 6

People swear, I know. Some of them swear a lot. I'm not averse to the odd curse word myself. Just so you know, it's all out there really, as I tell you this, but I've been largely editing out the cussing. Maybe you don't like swearing. Or maybe you don't think life sounds quite real without it. Oh well, I've started doing it now so I'll just carry on most likely. You can add your own favourites back in if you like. By the way, sorry it's been a few weeks. I've been a bit busy, but I'm back now. You know, I don't think I've even had a drink in two weeks. I don't drink at home as a rule. This pint is going to taste good, despite the circumstances.

"So just how long has it been since you last saw Dad?" My sister and I were sitting in the Red Lion, having lunch. Rachel had reluctantly agreed to meet me here, after having exhausted her usual run of excuses. We ended up having something more of a discussion than usual. I was on home territory after all and, though I could never describe myself as belligerent, I was at least more determined and curious with a pint in my hand. We also had something to talk about.
"Yeah, pretty recently," she says.
"What does that mean though? Your 'recently' and mine can differ somewhat."
"A few days. A week or so maybe. Not long."
"Since he burned his hand? Or before?"
"Er, well that would be before. Just before I think."
"You know he burned his hand, right?"
Rachel sighs. A time-honoured sign of one point to me.
"Ok, I didn't. You know I didn't."
"I'm not trying to win points here. I just need you to

understand what is going on."
She sits back and toys with her drink. It's a white wine spritzer, for God's sake. She looks a little drained I must say and I am in danger of feeling a little guilty. After an even deeper sigh she says, "Right, ok, what are we talking about here?"

So I give her the potted summary I had received from Dad and his doctor during our first visit to the clinic together. I mention dementia but avoid the dreaded 'A' word, which would only cause an overreaction, and no one is quite sure what exactly is going on just yet anyway.
"Thing is," I say, "he's like himself a lot of the time when I'm there. But then there are other times that he's not so well. He's all like dizzy and has trouble gathering his thoughts. He can even get a little angry. It's pretty scary first few times, but you kind of get used to it. You know, I can't believe how quickly this has happened. At least for us. I think Dad's been seeing this coming for a while now and keeping quiet about it."
Rachel stares at her drink but says nothing. She's searching for something to say. Fair enough. I've known a fair bit more than her, in the way of details, for weeks and I'm still searching for the right words myself. I'm not even sure there are any to find.
"It's hard to predict," I continue. "So the doctor just asked that, for now, *we*, that is you and me, check up on him as much as we can. Just to see that he is ok. Rach, we can't leave him for days, or weeks on end like we used to. That's the difference. He is going to sort out some visits from carers too if – when – the need arises. But he's going to need us as well." A sigh, then a sip. "Bit of a role reversal, eh?"
Rachel gives me this look. I expect it's like the one I gave Dad when I saw his note. She has gone from drained to

crushed in one move. That's the difference between wilful ignorance and final realisation. It's a big gap and it only works one way, on the whole.

"I didn't think it was *that* bad," she says. "Well I know you sort of told me…"

"I thought I *told you* told you."

"… but I didn't want to believe it and he seemed fine last time, so I just hoped, you know..."

Yes, I do know. "Well, he's not going to get better, that much is certain." I take another sip of my pint.

"Aren't there any drugs he can take or something? Any treatments?"

"Remarkably little, considering how prevalent the problem is. I'm afraid that hoping for a miracle cure is not going to get us anywhere, Rachel. If the doctors can help *us* when it's our time we should count ourselves lucky. It's just too late for Dad."

She takes a decent chunk out of her spritzer. I don't mean the ice cube. "I don't know what I can do. I'm a living breathing maid-cum-taxi service as it is. Football, scouts, karate, swimming. Parties on the weekend. School trips. It never ends. And I'm thirty five miles away, Dan."

I confess I'm not feeling particularly sympathetic here.

"You have a car. It's not that far."

"It's far enough when you've got no time left in your day as it is. The kids take up a lot of time, Daniel."

She rarely calls me Daniel, so I can tell she's upset. She's a strong one, though, so she won't show it if at all possible. This is just one of many traits we have never shared.

"Rachel, even I can't be there every day. You've got to help me out a bit. Cancel karate or something."

"I can't cancel karate! Ethan would go spare. It wouldn't be fair on him!"

I lift my hands like a human weighing scales.

"Karate or Dad. Karate or your *Dad*?" I say.

"It's not that simple, Dan! I've got responsibilities."
Ouch, that was a bit unfair. Well, ok, I don't have any responsibilities, this much is true, but that doesn't absolve her entirely. So I take another sip and say:
"Yes, and Dad is now going to have to be one of them. I'm sorry but you can't put this all on me, kids or no kids. I'll get you another."
Her glass is empty and I need to leave her to digest that last thought for a moment while I'm at the bar. I'm also avoiding further argument, having now gone well over my natural limit for such things, and I was suddenly conscious that our volume level was gradually rising. A few newspaper readers at the tables around us may have started to listen in.

While at the bar I reflect on how other societies look after their parents or grandparents, despite knowing virtually nothing on the subject. My imagination is immediately drawn to the Eskimos. But that is not a happy place to start. I don't even know if the story, you know the one, that they leave their old folk out in the cold to die, is even true. It can't be true now surely, not in this day and age? I don't know. So then my mind then swoops back over the Atlantic Ocean, across Europe and settles in the rural hills of Italy, where Rachel's wine is coming from as it goes, to a dining table in a garden surrounded by flowers and vines. It is a beautiful sunny day. A family is sitting there, all eating together, at least four generations represented, the old folk respected, laughing with the children, sharing a bowl of olives…

"That'll be £7.89, Dan, please."
"Good God, £7.89!? Oh yeah, the wine, the wine…" Don't get into a round with wine drinkers, by the way. You will always end up over-spending heavily. "There's a tenner. Cheers."

As I await my meagre change, I can see that my Italian idyll was possibly no truer today than the Inuit scenario. But I am still left with the feeling that we could be doing the whole family thing better in this country somehow. In our race for careers and mortgages we somehow seem to have forgotten how we are going to cope when things inevitably start to go wrong and we need to bring ourselves back together again. There are surely going to be big gaps in any family these days. Right now my sister and me are starting to feel the effect of our own gaps. Just as well I had already moved back home or I don't know what we'd do. Back at the table, Rachel is thumbing through her diary. I quickly hand her the spritzer. A cold glass just feels wrong in my hand.
"I think I can work something out. Once, maybe twice a week. It can't be for long though. I'll still have to get the kids sorted for school."
"Thanks Rach. Let's start from there and see how we go. Cheers." I give her a quick hug.
Rachel then starts to cry. I did that to her. That was me.

Bollocks.

After a while Rachel had to go. I decided to stay. You see, there was this woman sitting over nearer the bar who had caught my eye. About my age I guess, maybe a little older. I had noticed her a while back, mainly because she kept adopting the prayer position. I don't mean some weird tantric yoga stance or some such thing. I mean that she just kept holding her hands together under her chin. It made her look so serene and peaceful as she was reading her book or looking around the bar. I have had a few now, so I have to ask.

"I have to ask," I ask, "but are you actually praying? In a pub?" She parts her hands and looks me up and down, no doubt assessing how much of a tosser I was. I continue at haste. "Sorry, I'm not usually this blunt, but you know, you don't see that sort of thing much. In here I mean. I mean you probably see that in church and that and not so much drinking in there ha ha but…I'll shut up."

Oh dear, a severe case of foot in mouth again. Why does the consumption of a few pints always make me forget that I am so terribly prone to being like this?

She takes a drink, looks at her hands, then looks at me. Then, finally, she smiles.

"I get that a lot," she says. "Mostly from the god botherers who want to share my rapture or something. It's just…" she adopts the position again, "…a habit. I was only…thinking."

"Well it's very convincing." I say. "Sorry to be so unoriginal."

"That's not a problem. Nothing new under the sun eh? What's your name?"

"Er…Dan. Hello."

"Bernadette."

"Uh huh?"

"No laughter?"

"Er no. Should I be, er, laughing?"

"Bernadette, the praying atheist drunkard? Named after Saint Bernadette?"

"Er…"

"Saint Bernadette, who discovered visions of Mary…"

"You mean *that* Mary? I may have heard of her…"

"Yes!" she bangs a hand on the bar, grinning from ear to ear. "*That* one. That very one. Mary, Mother of God, no less. She has made several visits to earth since she assumpted…"

There's a new word. I'll have to let that go and check up on it later.

"…and so then she visited this girl in nineteenth century

France. Bernadette. And one hundred years later I get her name. To date, she has yet to visit me!"

"That really happened did it?" This is not my area of expertise, hence I'm treading carefully. You never know, I might learn something.

"Who knows? Enough people thought so for some reason. Lourdes is this whole industry now. For those who want miraculous healing and the like."

"Do you mean like 'throw away your crutches and walk again' type of thing? I can see how that might be a powerful idea in nineteenth cent…"

"Yeah, yeah that sort of stuff," says Bernadette dismissively, then points a finger at me. "Maybe she was onto something." Then her hand drops and she sighs. "I don't know, maybe she was just *on* something! Or maybe her brain was wired wrong. Whatever, whatever, either way, there's *some* room for amusement here surely?"

"Um, is this a Catholic thing? I'm not too familiar with the vagaries..."

"Oh yeah, it's a Catholic thing alright…" she declares, raising her glass. I can't tell what the hell is in it. "…the drinking, not the praying!" At that she laughs her head off, then abruptly stops. "You having another?" she asks and looks me dead in the eye.

There is only one answer to that question.

Drinkers I can handle. Women, under certain strict conditions, I can also handle. Even people who pray occasionally and don't ask me to do the same I can handle. But alcoholics? No, sorry, I can't handle them. It is entirely because it is too much like holding up a mirror up to what I could so easily become myself, if I don't watch out. Spending time with an alcoholic is conceptually just too close for comfort for me. And usually a little unpredictable too.

It takes me a short while to realise exactly what I have got myself into here. So it is with some distinct discomfort that I share another couple of drinks with Bernadette and watch her gradually slip down into depths I have never explored myself. There is something going on down there, something from her upbringing but she talks at me as if I know the whole story already and it fails to make any kind of coherent sense. It's not a happy place in there though, that much I do know. Soon enough she gets so wasted that I can hardly understand what she is going on about at all. Then the eyes start to wander in different directions and I decide this is doing no one any good. Neither of us is going to learn any more from this meeting and I don't want her latest bender to be on my conscience. I make my excuses and prepare to leave. She beats me to it, finishes her drink, slaps me on the shoulder, smiles and says goodbye. She's seen the signs from uncomfortable strangers before, I've no doubt. Then she strides out of the pub with all the dignity and self-control she can muster. I haven't seen her back at this pub since. Good luck to you Saint Bernadette. You are going to need it.

So I do know, in case you were wondering, that drink can be your enemy as well as your friend. I can be prone to a rose-tinted view of the world, I am aware of this, but I'm not stupid. I promise that this is *never* going to happen to me. And I sure hope with all my might it never happens to any of my friends. After all, imagine being told you could never drink again or you'd die? That would kill me. You may think I drink a lot, but I don't overall, not really, I promise. It's just that my sober moments are less interesting, so who wants to hear about them?

That last meeting may well have affected me a little though, and the next day I just wasn't in a sociable mood. We all get days like that though, don't we. It was the weekend, however, so after a fraught session at Dad's house, I still popped down the Lion for a bit, just to get out of the house. This time I sat in the far corner and kept myself to myself, while still watching those around me. It was a strange experience, like watching the television, because everyone else in there seemed to look right through me as if I wasn't there, even though I was just a table or so away. 'Invisible days' I call them, often characterised by you just not being able to get served at the bar when it's obviously your turn. Even though you are standing the same way you always do, even in the same place. Some days you just have this sort of demeanour that causes people to unconsciously ignore the hell out of you. The next day you could be feeling exactly the same and get served straight away, even though it's not your turn. Swings and roundabouts.

I should stress, though that if I'm *sure* that someone who was *definitely* before me needs serving, I would certainly let them get served first. That's just basic politeness and, for me at least, one of the rules of the pub. You can't always do this in practice, since things can get a little confusing up there. Also, letting someone in first sometimes can turn into a disastrous mistake. What I mean is that this can cause the bar person to presume that you are not in fact desirous of a drink at all at this juncture, thank you very much, and proceed to ignore you, even in favour of that day's 'Invisibles'. Thankfully, this is a rare thing in one as experienced as myself. Getting served at the bar is an art form in itself even on the best of days, and something you just have to pick up early in your drinking career. Drives foreigners mad, I would imagine.

I think it all stems from that other great British tradition, the round system. Buying a drink for each of your group must go back to ancient days, to secure alliances and stuff

like that, but now we just use it to confirm our friendships, however brief or shallow. It does provide a connection though, a debt. One for which repayment is expected, either that day or perhaps after years and years. And importantly, it's not just about the money. It's also about:
1. The getting up off your seat.
2. The going to the bother of getting the attention of the staff.
3. The remembering of the order.
4. The carrying it back.
5. The trying to get your seat back again.
Therefore asking someone else to go up to the bar when it is your round, waving a twenty pound note at them as if that makes it alright, is a big no-no. That does not constitute 'getting your round in'. Uh uh. No way. Also, in the long run, having the reputation for not 'getting your round in' makes you about as popular as a conscientious objector in wartime. Any serious pub-goer simply cannot allow this to happen to them. Ever.

Did you know, somewhere in my subconscious is a complex round-calculating system. It can work out who I owe, and who owes me, over virtually all the rounds I have ever been in ever. Very clever! Although not entirely precise. Its output, you see, is a little vague and the program (let's call it *Brit Round 1.0, Dan edition*) only sends out a vague notion of indebtedness, or otherwise, rather than an actual tally. Most people I know, though, seem to be running a similar program and amazingly it all seems to work out fine in the end. If I was at all religious I may be seriously wondering if purgatory is where you have to atone for all the pints you didn't buy someone. The punishment would be that you had to take a drink of something god-awful to make amends for every pint owed before you were allowed into heaven. Like Sambuca for example. Don't worry, this is just a mildly entertaining mid-pint musing, not an epiphany. As it goes, I really like the round system, even though today it's just a round of one. It's another part of the mad charm of the drinking culture here, a strange form of camaraderie. This also drives foreigners mad, I would imagine.

So who do we have here today, happily ignoring me and my pint? It is now that odd time, after the main afternoon session, but before the evening crowd really get going. This time of day is a *gap*, a space between. Neither one thing nor the other, neither fish nor fowl. Sorry, I'm getting carried away. What I mean is, anything can happen at this time. The alkies would probably be here, as they could be whenever. But you can also get the families here now, parents squeezing in an extra pint before they really, *really* have to take the kids home, reminiscing about the days that they would just stay out all day on a double session. You can get couples on early dates, perhaps tentative ones where you don't want to get too drunk, or for it to get too near bedtime. That way you can get away, just in case it goes wrong. There's a couple like that over there now. They've only been there for two drinks, but I think it is going well as they are leaning in now and the conversation is flowing, albeit mainly from him to her. Oh look, now they're holding hands! Jesus, they could be here for the evening too at this rate. Then there's those three retired gentlemen over by the door, discussing something loudly. Not in a bad way. It feels like politics possibly, but they are speaking in a foreign language so I can't really tell. I like that. It's good to get animated about something.

Then there's a group of people on the next table, five of them. They look like they should be out later, not now. At this time, in a parallel universe, in another quantum superposition, each of them, and all their atoms, will be back home getting ready for the night ahead, in front of a mirror, listening to Sigue Sigue Sputnik, or whatever gets them going. They, and their associated atoms, will be sending and receiving excited text messages, arranging the meeting time and place. 'Lion at 8!' or suchlike. Instead, in this universe, all their atoms are already here. They are three pints in for the fellas, and the wine equivalent for the two ladies. You see groups like this, by which I mean groups outside of their usual drinking time zone, all the time if you are looking. The reasons behind this are different on each occasion. But take a listen and you'll pick up why soon enough. I pick up my book and have a listen.

"Hang on, hang on. I'm just going to call my flatmate to check. I don't think I set it to series record."
"Numpty. Don't forget, I'm relying on you for that. I don't even have a box."
"I heard the rumours!" Laughter ensues. So far so mundane, but wait for it. It will come.
"You will never know, tosser. Well then, is she going to record it?"
"Hang on, I've only just sent the text."
"Who's round is it then?"
"Probably mine. I'll get them in. Same again?" Various versions of affirmative ensue.
"That's the kind of th…" Beep beep.
"Oh yeah, yeah. Oh, it was on series record, from the last time. Brill!"
"…the kind of…"
"Sweet. I'll be round yours to catch up tomorrow then. I'll bring a bottle!"
"…kind of thing…"
"A bottle? Bring two or I'm not letting you in!"
"This is the kind of thing I'm going to miss most."
"What's that then? Drinking with us?"

"The TV shows." Here it is, it's coming now. "For six months I'm going to miss *everything*. You just can't catch up on that much Eastenders."
"No sympathy. None at all. You're going off round the world, as you *keep* saying, and you're worried about what happening in Albert Square? Believe me, two days in and you won't give a damn about Watford, Walford, whatever, or, for that matter, any of us neither."
"Hey that's not true. I'll miss you guys. Damn right I will. And hey, and it's really great you are sending me off. I'm moved. Deeply moved." He then proceeds to belch, which is quite funny, I suppose. All that lager gas must have helped. And so there we have it, one of them is getting a send-off. I would imagine his flight is later tonight or early tomorrow, precluding the timing of a normal session.
"Miss us? Three days in Bangkok and you won't even remember your own name, never mind ours!"
"Here's to Bangkok."
"Bangkok!" Chink chink.
And so on.

There's only so much banter from other people's groups you can zone in on before it all seems a bit inconsequential. Don't get me wrong, I love the banter I engage in with *my* friends. I can do it for hours. I live for it to some degree. Naturally, *we* talk about much more interesting and amusing things than soap operas and set top boxes, well sometimes anyway, but I expect that from an outside perspective our conversations sound equally dull and vacuous. As I casually sip down through my next pint the send-off group continues through their round at a great pace. Then the evening crowd start to fill the place up, turning the pub familiar again. The couple have gone. The debaters are still there and are still debating. I sure hope this off-on-his-travels guy, now on some dreadful looking shot, doesn't forget when his flight is. However, I shall never know, as it is on the wrong side of busy now for my current state of mind. I chug down the last of my pint in one go and place the empty glass on the bar on my way out. Early night tonight for me.

CHAPTER 7

I have had another conversation with Dad's doctor. Dad has been discussing his condition with him for a quite a while now it transpires. He was Mum's doctor too, as it goes. They have known each other for years so apparently have this easy rapport, even over the most cruel and fundamental aspects of life. Doctor Roberts is becoming increasingly concerned about Dad's mental well-being and wants to know how much more help myself and Rachel are able to give him. I gave him a fair assessment of what I could do and asked him why, how much is he going to need? Doctor Roberts replied by saying that Dad possibly has quite an aggressive instance of the condition but it was too early to tell etc etc. He then said we should think about making plans while we could. I have no idea what all this actually means. I can't blame the doctor, he can only tell us what he can be sure of and I guess this is one big grey area for him. It must be different every time, but each occasion equally depressing.

However, I find myself musing, for me this problem with Dad exists in the present, not in the future when things get bad. It exists right now, as this thing in my life, when before it just didn't. It wasn't there at all. Now it is. Like from black to white, or vice versa more likely. Matter itself, I have read, the very stuff our bit of the universe is made of, can similarly just come from nothing, then disappear to nothing again. In fact it does this all the time, and Dad's condition has done the same. Dad's condition is not going to disappear again though, that's for sure. Bugger this, I'm going to the pub.

And while I was on my own in there for a while, I caught myself still musing over the possibilities around what the doctor had said. The best and the worst, none of which were satisfactory. This was obviously not going to be good therapy so I quickly changed the subject on myself and instead began to work out how many hours of my life I had spent doing certain things. You know, like some articles you read in someone else's magazine from time to time. So I started to work out how many hours I had spent:

1. In a Jacuzzi
2. Watching telly
3. Having a crap
4. Having sex
5. Working

After about half a pint I gave up on working out the actual hours. That was too hard. And no one was going to be marking my work. So I ended up just summarising as follows:

1. Not enough.
2. Probably too much.
3. About right.
4. Definitely not enough.

As for 5, I definitely spend too much of my time at the office, that's for sure. I have taken to bringing in another copy of that book on Quantum mechanics to work with me. This is so I can keep up with Dad during our inevitable discussions on the subject. Dad still has mine so I got this one out of the library. It's quite a difficult read when you are nodding off in bed, so it seems better to dip in during the daylight hours. I confess I don't really understand much of it second time round either, but it does, at least, make me think. Which is how I usually like to go about things.

Anyway, one day last week, I was reading about a deterministic view of the universe while I had my morning cup of tea. This blew my mind a little so I had to dumb down the idea a bit, to fit it into my brain. Imagine that the Big Bang set every particle in the universe into motion and all that is happening now is just that one push still unfolding, still moving every particle in the direction it always had to go, based on the force and position of everything right at the very start. A bit like breaking off in a game of pool. Stay with me here. Once you strike the cue ball there's nothing else you can do. The speed, angle, and position of the cue ball, even the amount of dust or beer stains on the cloth, all contribute to create the exact position of all the balls following the shot. Right? And it's different every time no matter how hard you try to make it the same. So here we all are, still just sitting in the universe as one of the 'balls' flying round, unable to change the shot or the outcome. We are after all, completely made of tiny particles of matter, all shot out from the singularity at the dawn of existence. Bit depressing. Hmm, ok but that doesn't seem right to me instinctively. For example, I'm pretty sure that I just decided to actually decide to have a cup of Earl Grey this morning, as opposed to my usual English Breakfast. That, intuitively, did not feel like product of the Big Bang.

As I later read on I find that Quantum Mechanics fundamentally requires chaos and an element of the unknown, so this determinism is probably not right anyway. It seems that we can only ever predict probabilities. And I suppose that with probabilities come possibilities. Then with possibilities come choices. So much for pool balls then. Reassured, I put the book down and decided to do some work.

Later though, I get the nagging feeling that life now would be easier if my life was just the movement in the middle of a pool shot, unburdened of all these pesky choices.

So, as you eagle-eyed may have gathered, I do actually have a job. I might have mentioned it sooner but it didn't feel as important as anything else I've told you just yet. People always want to know about your job though. Sometimes that's the first thing they ask of you, or offer to tell you. Like that is the main part of their life that defines them. Soon enough, after the first hello or hand shake there's always the 'What do you do?' question. My answer should be 'Well mostly I come in here' but social convention tends to force us to exchange mind-numbing irrelevancies about our current employment before we can really get on to the interesting stuff. I mean, what's wrong with 'Hi, I'm Dan. I like a beer and a chat. No kids. Not really bothered about Star Wars or Star Trek as it goes but I love Billy Bragg'. And so on. It's as good a start as any.

You occasionally get to meet someone who has an interesting job, or at least a passion for their choice of employment. This is not me, but I had better just tell you the basics in case you are curious. It's not really what I went to University for, I admit. I could blame having to leave my life in London, and tell you a tale of sacrificing my career for the good of the family. That would not be true though. Would you actually think better of me if it was? As it goes, I was going nowhere there in the capital, really. All those half-hearted ambitions just seemed to dissolve in the face of my apathy. Maybe apathy is a bit strong. I was just too neutral, I think, living for the weekend, and never thinking ahead. And so fast-forward a bit. Here I am, in an office, doing mid-range work on spreadsheets. Not too boring, not too stressful. It could be worse. Right, enough of that. If I tell you much more about my work day I expect you will just up and leave. Ok, just one thing then. I'll be quick.

Yesterday's time in the office was initially spent with a heavy two hours on Excel, but I felt I had earned a little break. I don't smoke so I don't think I get the same sort of breaks as the smokers. Therefore, I think it's perfectly fine and fair to sit at my desk and have a read for a bit instead. I was reading about Quantum Tunnelling today. This is another strange concept but I shall try my best to explain.

Imagine an electron bombing around like it does, allowing your hairdryer or your neurons to work as you have come to expect. Sometimes it needs to change its, what should I call it, its energy state. Er, think of this as like trying to get up a hill. You just need to have enough energy to get to the top, then you are ok, right? Any cyclist would understand. But it seems that if an electron gets a bit tired halfway up the conceptual hill of changing energy states, then it can just borrow a bit of energy required from the universe around it, then tunnel through the hill to get to the other side. Then it just gives the energy back. Are you still with me here? Maybe it's a bit like a pay day loan but without the equally mind-blowing interest payments. So, anyway, these particles can *cheat*, that's the thing. They don't have to run their lives by the same rules we do. But I'm *made* of electrons, and other subatomic particles! This does not seem fair. I stare at the wall to the world outside and try to sum up the energy to break through it. The wall is virtually all empty space after all. But where am I going to borrow energy from? I sigh and look around. From nothing round here, that's for certain. This place is an energy vacuum. Not literally, you understand. The smokers are heading back now, so with a sigh I put the book down and get back to it. 'It' being work.

I have a boss of sorts, Brian he is called. I'm pretty self-sufficient and get enough done generally, so he seldom has to bother me. I see my primary job here is to keep things just like that, mainly because he is a bit of a bully to everyone else in his path. Thankfully I'm back in spreadsheet heaven when he walks past my desk, a little too close, clearly within those boundaries of personal space. I work hard at ignoring him. I take inspiration from a sparrow I watched in my garden last weekend, going about its manic business as a swan gracefully flew by. How would that sparrow feel if it did look up at that moment? Impressed? Jealous possibly? Shit scared even? Or not much at all. It takes me a while before I realise Brian has stopped and has actually been trying to get my attention. It's time for the weekly meeting, for God's sake. A worthless use of the time of all concerned, but we seem to have to keep doing this for some reason. Solely for the lack of an alternative idea as far as I can tell.

You don't want to see the official meeting minutes. These were *my* meeting notes though:
Words. Don't they just spill and spill out of people's mouths? Where do all of these words come from? God, this meeting is interminable. Time is not a constant.

As it goes, time is *not* a constant. It depends on how fast you are travelling. And gravity. From the top deck of the bus on the way home, though, you can't tell the difference.

On the subject of job satisfaction, later that evening, sitting at the bar of the Red Lion, I found some distraction in the life of Gareth. He is, for now at least, a local criminal lawyer. I've met him before, but he's more of a casual acquaintance than an actual acquaintance. He has to frequent all sorts of pubs, he told me once, when meeting certain clients of his. The Red Lion, surprisingly, is rather nicer than his usual haunts, and provides less risk of bumping into any clients in a non-professional capacity. This is somewhat reassuring, I suppose, but at least he must have picked up some great tales to tell after spending time with that lot. However, I'm not about to head to The Swan for a pint to check that out any time soon. Maybe I am a bit of a snob, maybe I'm just being sensible. Gareth, I notice, is being a bit more drunk than usual. I only had to ask him 'What's up?' and he was off like a rocket.

"Just so you understand, this isn't true, right? If this was true then I couldn't actually tell you any of this."

"Er, right…"

"Client confidentiality."

"Right."

"So none of this happened. And the names are different."

I take a sip. "Got it."

"But it's got me thinking if I'm not in the wrong job. Which is why I fancied a pint."

"I'm with you. Fire away."

"Right. So, imagine if there was this girl, a woman really. She's in a bad relationship. He beats her up and all that."

"I know, the things you have to deal with. I don't know how you do it. So he was the one that is-definitely-not your client?"

"No, no. I mean actually *no,* not him. Anyway, after some years, far too long, but hey figure that one out, she not only leaves him but weaves this intricate story of emigrating to Australia. To stop him following her, you know."

"Ok, that's sounds extreme, but inventive. I take it that this fictional lady does not end up in Australia?"

"No, she moves here, about thirty miles away from where they lived together."

"That sounds a bit risky. Not living here I mean. I mean not moving that far. It stands to reason, she could easily bump into him at some point, right?"

"Uh huh. Two years later she did just that. Outside the butchers. He was fine though, just then, said he had changed, and all that. That time he just talked, said sorry and left. Trouble is, after that he started stalking her didn't he. He would keep turning up round her house and her office. Said he wanted her back. She told him not to come back. She is stronger now, but she's still scared."
"I see. But stalking is an offence now, right? So this is where you definitely-did-not come in then."
"No, no. The real trouble was that this guy had a new girlfriend." He turns and looks at me. "How can these bastards just keep attracting all these women? Makes no sense to me."
"I have mused on that very same subject myself, Gareth. This needs further research."
We are almost empty, but handily we are at the bar, so I politely wave over for a couple of more pints without disrupting his flow.
"Hmm, anyway, his current girlfriend gets suspicious and starts stalking *him*. After a while she spots him with our original lady."
"Who must have wished she *was* in Australia by now."
"Perhaps. Anyway, the new girlfriend only ignores him and leaps on the old girlfriend. Really lays into her. She's a lovely piece of work, that one, by the way. Kicking, scratching, punching. Some colourful language too apparently."
"And where is our hero at this point in this tale?"
"Oh, he has buggered off at this point. Hasn't been found since as it goes. In the story I mean. Thanks mate." He takes a decent gulp of his new pint. He likes a Guinness, if you care to know.
"So the new girlfriend was your not-client then?"
He takes another sip, and shakes his head. I'm going to have to stop second guessing this story.

"Oh no. *She* was the one who pressed charges. The first girlfriend had to bite her on the arm to get her off, see."
"Yeah, but self-defence right? Jesus!"
"Jury didn't think so." Gareth checks his watch. "Right now she is being transferred to her first night in prison. Meanwhile that bitch, sorry, but it's true, is no doubt having a party, bragging about how she sorted 'that posh cow' out, and our hero is probably chatting up his next victim right now in some bar somewhere."
"Sounds rough," I say. "Glad it's not true." I notice that rather than changing any names, he just managed to do without them entirely, but I let that lie.
Gareth stares at his pint and sighs. "I'm at least 25 years from retirement. That's a long time." He stretches out the 'long' into something rather, well, long. It sounds like a lament. No, it *is* a lament.
It's at times like this that I don't mind my job so much after all.

This all brings to mind an article I was reading in a magazine Amy passed my way a few weeks ago, when she nipped out to the shops for five minutes (think twenty five) and asked me to look after her drink. It was one of those lifestyle magazines I wouldn't normally touch with someone else's barge pole, but said she reckoned I would like it, and anyway it would keep me company until she got back. Like I needed that. Anyway, it was based on an interview with a stroke victim and his wife. Don't worry, it wasn't too depressing. In fact, it was a little heartening in a way. You see, this guy used to be a big City lawyer. You know, working at a top firm looking after the big corporations and the big money, that sort of thing. He was good at it too, a partner at a relatively young age and personally in the big money leagues himself. They had a good life in some ways, his wife explains, but he was never really there, by which she means at home. He seemed always to be at work, and when he was at home he was always checking his email, or on the phone. She got used to it, she says, but it made her a little sad. He didn't mind at all, he says, not at the time. Ever since joining the firm, straight out of university, he had to work hard to keep up, and the hours and the obsession soon became normal. It just became what his life was, what normal life was, and he became surrounded by people who thought the same. The rest of the world just faded out of view. He never said that last bit. That was me paraphrasing as I grabbed another pint and returned to the article.

Everything changed when he had a stroke. A pretty big one by all accounts, and by his own account, without warning. As I read on, I suspect there actually were warnings, but he chose to ignore them as he skipped from meeting to meeting. But there's no way to tell for sure. He took a long time to recover, and there's a few paragraphs on that subject, which I skip over a bit, but the point was that even when he was relatively well again he never recovered his short term memory, or the ability to make new memories. I turn the page and this quote appears above a picture of the couple, sitting by the lake, in big print:
"I've never been happier."
I raise an eyebrow or two and take another swig. Maybe Amy was on to something after all. It turns out that losing his short term memory meant that he had no chance whatsoever of returning to his old job. A lawyer like him lives on the ability to take in new information and use it for the benefit of their clients. So he was given a party, a handshake and a payoff then had to leave. In the article, he proceeds to explain that this is where his life actually began, not ended.
"There's so many things I can't do anymore because of the

memory loss, but I have so much time for other things now instead. All I thought about before was work, so much so that I forgot to imagine that there was even anything else, that there could be another life for me out there. But there is! I now volunteer for a local helpline. I can't remember anything after the call but they record them anyway and I can give advice on things I knew about from before the stroke. And we both spend much more time in our cottage by the lake, and just enjoy life!"

The churlish part of me can't help but think that that's ok for him, having the money set aside to have a cottage by a lake, and work without getting paid and all that, but it's a positive tale nonetheless. I read on. His wife said:

"There are a lot of problems of course. I can't leave him on his own for too long or he may get confused. And he always carries his notebook with him to leave notes for himself as he can't retain anything that has just happened for long. But we've never been happier."

The article carries on in this vein for a while, with a few obvious before and after pictures to accompany the text, so as not to scare off the usual readership. Hugs and smiles to the camera. The article finishes with this:

"What a fool I was, needing to have a stroke to wake up to living my life!"

Indeed. I looked at my watch, decided that Amy will be back in a minute, and got us both another drink. I decided to get us each a pint of Jon Porridge, 4.0%, purely for the name. Shortly afterwards she burst in, a little out of breath, with a couple of bags and a brief apology. She grabbed back the magazine.

"Sorry, sorry. Read it, did you? Interesting, eh, don't you think?"

"Yeah, not bad. Better than I was expecting, I admit. Shame he needed something that drastic to wake up to

himself."
"Yeah, the brain's a freaky thing, and no mistake."
"Yes, that did seem to be the main thrust of the piece."
Then we talked about something else by and by. I never gave the article a second thought until just now.

CHAPTER 8

It may surprise you to know that I don't get hangovers. Not as a rule anyway. I'm pretty sure this is not a sign of a drinking problem. It is more so that I have, by now, found out what agrees with me and as a rule steer clear of all else. The uninterrupted consumption of 'proper beer', and only that, results in no headaches ever. If I move onto the shorts, however, then I'm in trouble. Cigars are also a bad sign of a night going awry. Importantly, I also now know when to stop, a skill that every serious pub-goer needs to acquire at some point. That ability to still hear your subconscious saying 'That'll do' over the cacophony of the late night boozer, and turn on your heels and head home before you can change your mind. It took years for me to pick up that particular ability. Recovery periods are also a good idea. They make you appreciate the next session. I should run a course on this stuff, I really should.

I also have a theory, bear with me, that everyone has their happy drink and, conversely, everyone has their sad drink. You know, that 'sad' drink that you can just have a tiny little bit of and it sends you loopy, even when you could have drunk four times the amount of anything else? Most people I know have one. Do not get Amy on whisky for example, or be prepared to clear the area. But on Vodka she can just keep going and going, and be entirely personable. Gin, historically, is supposed to be everyone's sad drink. I don't agree, but I just don't like the taste. Don't like tonic much either so that pretty much does me in for a G&T. Anyway, quite by accident I found out that Tequila is my happy drink. Then I also found out that there is a limit to just how much happiness a man can take. Lager is my sad drink. Sometimes though, you end up in a bar with no proper beer and have to go for a lager. Then I get a bit maudlin, apparently, and then I get a hangover. Which makes conversations like this all the more difficult.

Dad says, "I've been reading these articles. Medical, you know. Can't remember much so I highlight bits I like. Look, there's this one guy who says 'where there's any little bit of hope, I'm going to grasp it. I'm never going to give up fighting'. Laudable for sure."
"Laudable, for sure. What a guy." I agree.
"I'm just not that guy."
I let that sink in for a moment. "No. Me neither," I offer.
"Why does everyone have to be a fighter anyway?"
I leave that there and go into Dad's kitchen to put the kettle on. When I'm back he is gone. He's still there, I mean, but I can see in his eyes that his brain has gone, for the moment at least. I sit and wait for him to come back. It's like staring at a stranger.

Sometime later, and Old Dad, by which I mean the Dad how Dad always used to be, has returned, sipping on a cup of tea and having a Malted Milk. I'm just sitting there quietly with my tea, a little unsure of the situation. He is being stoically pragmatic, therefore somewhat back in normal character.
"I don't want you sitting there grieving for me while I'm still here," he says. "How bad would that be for all of us? No, I am not going to put you through any more of this than necessary. Look here, I spent twenty years trying to keep you two safe and happy, until you left and had to sort that out for yourself. I was proud of that job. Me and your Mum both were. And you two have turned out fine. You're good people. So... So I'm not going to finish the job off by giving you years of pain and misery."
"It's ok, Dad. We'll manage," I offer weakly.
"Managing. And to what end may I ask?"

"I don't know, for the good times we might still have?"
He takes an appreciative bite of his biscuit. "Fine, for now, but once they are gone…"
"Dad…"
"Dan, when I'm not *me* any more I don't want to be anyone else, a shadow of myself. Once the *me* is gone I want to be properly gone."
"Dad, I don't know what you are asking of me."
"Just be there for me when the time comes."
I don't even know what that means, but I choose not to ask. Instead I nod.
"Remember the rabbit you told me about?"
"The mixi one? Yeah…"
"You were brave then, Dan. That poor thing needed putting out of its misery and you went over there and did the right thing. That can't have been easy."
Ok, *ok*, I may have embellished that story somewhat, but you can't go back on such lies once they are out there. It was only supposed to be a harmless story to give that poor bunny the ending that it deserved, the one in reality that it never got, ok? Jesus, and now Dad thinks I'm some kind of euthanasia hero. What exactly did I tell him again? I can't remember exactly. That's the problem with lying.
"It wasn't easy, no." I admit. "But that was different."
"Not from where I'm sitting, son. Not from where I'm sitting."
I've had enough of this, so I snap, just a little. Don't judge me, we all have our breaking points. "Ok, then Dad. Just how would you like me to kill you then?"
"Well, I…"
"Go on then, you must have thought about it. How should I go about this exactly?"
He shrugs his shoulders and says, "I have concentrated more on the principle than the practicalities, I admit…"
"Yes, well it's the practicalities are bothering me. How's

about…let me think… how's about I hold you down and smother you with a pillow?" I suggest.
"Oh you…"
"Hold you down until you stop struggling?"
"I don't think I'd like that. I don't think I'd like that at all."
"Me neither," I say.
"No, don't do that to me."
"Don't worry. I won't."
I have no idea why we are both smiling at this point. Maybe it's the old cliché that otherwise we'd cry.

Looking to change the subject, I ask him how he's getting on with the Quantum Mechanics book. He goes off to bring it back here then starts flicking through it for inspiration. I expect he's having trouble remembering the details now but doesn't want to tell me.
"Ah, here it is," he says. "My favourite bit, the Dual Slit Experiment."
"Yeah, I remember that bit. I started that bit thinking that I understood everything thus far, then ended the chapter wondering what the living heck was going on. What did you make of it?"
He takes another flick through the pages. "Yes, yes. I get the fact that if you drop sand through two slits in a piece of card you will get two piles of sand underneath the slits."
"Not a problem, that bit."
"And I can imagine that if you shine light through the same card you will get the waves of light interfering with each other and creating these peaks and troughs on a screen behind."
"Yup, I was pretty much happy with that too."
"I was even happy with the scenario where you dropped individual photons to the card and they would behave like light waves, even if they were actual particles, like grains of sand…"

"Hmm, I was starting to get lost a bit by then."

"…but it was the bit where if you added a detection device between the card and the screen that really got me."

"Er, remind me?"

"Well, if you had this detection device switched on, the photons behaved like the sand particles and formed two piles. If you switched it off, then the patterns formed by the photons on the screen reverted back to the peaks and troughs of a wave again."

"Ah yes, I remember. Spooky isn't it?"

"It's like these particles *know* when they are being observed and change their behaviour when they are. It's like they are *conscious*."

"Yeah, but they can't be conscious really. Can they? It is us who change our behaviour when we are being watched. And we consist of a lot more particles than one!"

"Hmm. I'd love to know what the answer is though." He looks different now. For the first time, it looks like he now had no expectation of finding out the answer anymore.

"Me too, me too. And do you remember the other thing?"

"The other…?"

"Where before the particle hits the screen it actually goes through both slits at the same time?"

"Right, right. Yes, I loved that idea! It goes through both, at least conceptually, but it's only when it hits the screen and we can see where it actually does hit, and therefore which slit it actually went through, that the other pathway collapses out of existence. Until then it's following both paths."

"You couldn't make it up could you? I wish *we* could try two paths at once and then pick the best one at the end."

"Hmm. But what if there isn't a best one?" Dad puts the book down and sighs. It would always be me who would signal an end to the lesson sessions, but now these roles are reversing. Shame, this would have been a really interesting thing to talk about.

We watch a bit of TV and Rachel comes round after a time. It's not her day but she was passing, she said. I put the kettle on and we carry on watching this war film. It's a Tuesday afternoon after all. Dad is too young to have been in the war so he has no war stories of his own. Rationing stories he does have, but these are more of a curiosity and are not a good basis for a matinee movie, judging by the output of the film studios. Meanwhile, on screen, some brave soldiers are shooting Germans and escaping to the border or something.
"That's not how it happened!" Dad shouts. "This is bullshit!"
He throws his mug at the screen but misses and it hits the wall. Thankfully it is not one of our favourites. And, also thankfully, it is now empty. Tea stains are very stubborn. Rachel and I just stare at each other in shock for a moment. Dad stands up and starts ranting at the screen, and he proceeds to tell us what it really was like. Except this isn't *him*. It is this fictional character that has now come into our lives, distinctly uninvited. I hardly ever saw him get angry before all this started, and never this angry. Well, maybe a little, like when he told Rachel off during her stroppy teenager years, but not like this. It is Rachel who reacts first. She just gets up and gives him a hug. The mothering instincts kicking in I expect. I move in and give him a good old British pat on the shoulder. Don't judge me, it was the best I could do in the moment. After a time he calms down, and takes his seat again. No one knows what to say for a few minutes. I go and pick up the various pieces of mug and sit down again. Then Dad says this:
"I'm sorry."
Protestations ensue immediately from me and Rachel of

course. But it didn't look like he was listening. He's a proud man in his own way and he wanted to take on the weight of the apology for us. That was all he had left to do, I suppose.

Two days later, I told him he had nothing to be sorry about. He looked at me blankly then blithely agreed before changing the subject. He's pretending to remember what I'm talking about again. I can recognise the signs already.

This all colours my mood as I head off out to my date. Yes, you heard me right. I'm off out on a date. It's been so long since the last one I had I can't remember how or why I made a mess of it. I don't intend to raid those memories again so I'm just going to wing it this evening. Emma is a work friend of Amy's and very nice apparently. Amy has basically fixed us up and neither of us, evidently, has had the strength to fight her over it. Amy is usually happy to leave me alone in this regard so there must be some reason why she has made the effort this time. Maybe Emma is in a bad place and needs some cheering up? No, that can't be right. Amy wouldn't have fixed her up with me in that case, surely. Maybe she thinks I need cheering up? No, she should know me well enough now not to choose the 'date' method of improving my existence. I'd rather just spend the time with her. Hey, you never know, she might think that we will actually like each other. Hmm. There's a whole load of pressure right there then. Oh well, off I go.

I suggested to Amy that we, i.e. myself and Emma, should just go out for a drink. Amy shook her head at me mournfully, and said that I should pick a restaurant. I then started thinking which one may be the most appropriate, but I must have been thinking for too long as eventually Amy calmly suggested the Italian off the High Street. Somewhat out of my comfort zone, I was relieved enough to agree immediately. So I'm standing outside there now, a little early, looking in the window. Emma's not there yet, unless the photo I have is massively inaccurate. And she has turned up with some spare bloke and two spare kids. Me being first is no surprise. Emma would not want to turn up there first and attract too much attention from the waiters and other diners. I shall have to do that instead. Ok, deep breath – I'm going in.

Once I am seated, pleasantries are exchanged with the staff. Assurances, from me, as to the undoubtedly impending arrival of my fellow diner are also completed, followed by knowing nods, and I am left alone to check the menu. I turn it around to look at the wine list. Or at least the beer part of the wine list. It is sadly lacking. An Italian lager or an Italian lager. Or the same Italian lager on draught. Oh dear, I may have to go for the wine after all.
"Dan? Is it Dan? It is you…er…are you feeling ok?"
I must have been screwing my face up in disapproval at the menu as Emma walked in unnoticed (by me) and then arrived at the table. I quickly change my face shape into a panicked smile and stand up. I stick out my hand. We shake hands. Was that right or not? Too formal? Oh well, too late now. On to second impressions already.
"Emma? Yes, no I'm fine. I was just, er. No, I'm alright. Hello!" is my opening line. Good start.

You're probably expecting me to say that this date was a disaster, and are looking forward to the gory details. It wasn't like that, really. It was ok. It was fine.
"No offence, but Amy virtually made me come out tonight." It was Emma who said that. I was thinking the very same thing, but chose not to vocalise it myself, thinking that Emma may indeed find this offensive. I do not happen to find this offensive, luckily for Emma.
I smile and say, "Yes, but I find it's best not to argue when

she has her mind set on something. It's been the case since we were sharing toys in nursery."

"Ha, you've known her that long? What was she like then?"

"I'm not sure I remember properly to be honest. I may be layering my later experiences onto the earlier memories."

She looks at me quizzically. "What do you mean?"

"You know. I may be remembering the four year old Amy, not as she was then, but as I know her to be since then. Yeah?"

"No idea what you mean. You remember or you don't right?"

I'm not going to debate the issue before even the starters arrive. We've already had to debate the wine choice then elect to have our different separate bottles. Mine's a Valpolicella, hers a Pinot Grigio. If I have to do wine, I'm going for red. White wine is just a step too far.

"Yeah, I remember her. I remember her," I elect to say. "Bossy then, bossy now. But a good mate."

"She's a great laugh at work. Well, by the mid-morning anyway. After a coffee or two. She's not a morning person, is she? Not at all."

"I wouldn't know. She's definitely an evening person. That I can be sure of."

"So what do you do, then?"

Oh.

I proceed through the standard work routine on autopilot for ten minutes or so, also concentrating on sipping my wine, and not quaffing it like a beer. I continue the script, leave pauses, and wait for the conversation to take a more interesting turn. The main course arrives. I have a pizza, she has a pasta dish. This is not a sign or a symbol. I like pasta too.

"So why did you end up back here, no offence?" Emma

asks. "You must have had a much more interesting job in London. You did used to live in London right?"
"Yes, you have been briefed correctly. No, not necessarily. You can get rubbish jobs there too, if you look hard enough." I'm thinking this is me being playful, a kind of a joke. I look up at Emma. Apparently not.
"So how come you ended up back here? I'll be going the other way as soon as I get the chance."
"Er, well it's a bit sad but…" take a sip, "but, my Mum died and I came back to be nearer Dad."
"Wow, that's good of you. I don't think I could have done that."
"No, it's nothing really. I was kind of sick of it anyway."
"How so? What's that they say? If you are sick of London you are sick of life?"
"Tired."
"Eh?"
"Tired of London. If you are tired of London, etc. Samuel Johnson said that."
"Right."
"But that was over 200 years ago."
"Really."
"Before the internet."
"Right."
"And online shopping."
"I get it. It's still got to be better than round here though."
I take a bite of my pizza. I have had better pizza in London. I have had worse too. After a gap I decide I should carry on the conversation.
"It depends on your point of view, I suppose." I elect to say, in lieu of silence, my normal stop-gap.
Emma's eyes light up. She's found a favoured topic in her head somewhere. "Hey, what shows did you see when you lived there? Did you see Les Miserables? Ooh, I love that show, just *love* it. I'd go and see that one again and again.

I'd go and see them all! Did you see Phantom? Did you see Blood Brothers?"
I had seen the first one mentioned, as it goes, and a handful of others, so we swapped some experiences on that subject for a while. Which, like I said, was fine.

As our respective bottles get similarly emptier, and the sips get bigger and more frequent, the evening gets easier. Emma opens up somewhat and tells me a lot about her sister. There are some jealousy issues there or something like that. Rachel and me were not competitive like that. Maybe because we had gender differences, it also meant that we had fewer actual differences.
"Alice was just so competitive, you know?" Emma says.
"Right."
"So she just *had* to take charge for Gran's funeral, didn't she? Mum was so tired and Dad was a little er, withdrawn by then, see. It was Mum's Mum by the way."
"Right. Sorry about that."
"S'ok. We were younger then. Grown up, but younger. Alice just breezed in though, after Gran died. She lived in Scotland, see? Alice I mean."
"Scotland. Right. Long way." I say, steering clear of controversy.
"So she's hardly been there when Gran was ill. I think she felt guilty and so tried to save some face by organising the funeral and probate and stuff. That was really bloody annoying. It was me and Mum who had to deal with everything all those months beforehand. After she lost her marbles. We had to look after her every single day in the end. And put up with the shouting and arguments and stuff. Alice didn't want to deal with any of that."
I look at her. I have a choice to make here. Emma's talking to the ceiling fan, really, not me. Would she be interested in my story? Would we find any solace in sharing our stories,

the chance to dilute the loneliness of the experience? I let her talk for a while, but when the gap comes I fill it with this:
"Shall we go for desert then?"
Doesn't seem the right time or place, somehow.

We do go for dessert and even try a piece of each other's. We talk about the Red Lion, amongst other things.
"You drink there too? I don't know what Amy see's in that place."
"You get good beer in there. Which should be the point largely, right?"
"Suppose. But you get all sorts in there. People I mean."
"That is also the point. Some of those all sorts are me, Emma."
She laughs at this. I think it must be the Pinot. "I see, well maybe I'll come join you down there sometime. When it's safe." Pause. "They sell wine, right?"
"I believe so. All the colours."
"Ha. All the colours! Funny. That's sorted then. Cheers."
We chink glasses. The bottles are empty and have already been removed. Neither of us can finish our last glass though.

We share the bill and head out of the restaurant in due course. Several other couples are finishing up too, so I think we managed to successfully fill the allotted time required to comply with the definition of 'date'. We exchange a kiss on the cheek and say we will do this again sometime. This may not happen, but it would be too rude of either of us to say so at this point.

The following morning I do have a bit of a hangover. Right on the front of the forehead. That's red wine for you.

CHAPTER 9

Amy has decided, again, that I need cheering up. Like that's going to help. For some inexplicable reason this is going to involve a day out in London. What have I done to deserve this, I wonder? We are going on a pub crawl and for some reason this is going to involve cocktail bars. Really, *what* have I done?

Neither she nor Jez are giving me any details. I don't think Jez knows any more than me to be honest. He's not the type to worry about the details. All I do know is that we are not going to visit *any* tourist spots at all, and there will be absolutely no shopping. Also, since this is a pub crawl it will involve at least three different drinking establishments. Amy did not actually specify this last point though. These are just the rules.

That's why I don't think I could live in a village that has just one or two pubs. You run out of places to crawl to before the end of the evening. Ok, I know I spend 90% of my drinking time in The Red Lion but the possibility of having somewhere else to go to, should the whim take you, is of great comfort. Plus, there's something more exciting about a pub crawl. It involves timescales, organisation and cooperation. A team effort, as it were, a bonding thing. But, like I said, it has to be at least three pubs or it doesn't count.

Once, me and Jen worked out that you could, if you were organised enough, go on a pub crawl for twenty-four hours straight in London. You would have to use the late bars in the West End and, for the early hours, the East End pubs open for the meat workers, postmen and the like, but it was doable. We bought a copy of Time Out and a map of

London and planned it all out in our living room. We were even going to arrange teams and do it all for charity and so on. It never happened though. Neither of us just had that spark to take it off the page and into real life. It would have been great fun if we had done it though, I'm sure. It was pretty good fun just planning it. It's too late now, on several levels. These days it just wouldn't have any novelty value. With changes to licencing laws, it would be just too easy to do now, which takes all the fun out of the idea. Not that I'm complaining, though, don't get me wrong.

"A family rail ticket? Seriously?"
Me and Jez are standing back as Amy buys our tickets. She is thoroughly in charge of proceedings today. Even more than usual, I mean. I continue.
"How can we get a *family* rail card? You won't pass as my Mum."
She turns round and eyes me up. "You two could pass as my Dads then."
"My Dad's what?" quips Jez. He's quick on the draw today. He's obviously terribly excited about today's plans.
"Shut up, it's not really a family ticket. It's a Group Super Saver or something. What does it matter anyway? It's the cheapest way to get to London and back. We just have to travel together, that's all."
"So we had best not lose you then," I say.
"I'm sure we'll manage. As long as no one pulls today we'll be ok!" she laughs.
"Yeah, in that case I think we will manage," Jez says to me. "Statistically, it seems likely."
"Fine, fine," I say. I don't know why I'm getting irate. Maybe I'm worried about being so far away from Dad for the day, even though it's one of Rachel's days. Maybe I don't like having fun forced upon me. Maybe I'm a tosser.

Amy hands the tickets over, we put them through the barriers then she collects them back again. No one argues, since she is absolutely in the right. We mosey along to the platform and wait for the train. Eight minutes, no delays.
"What now then?" Amy smiles mischievously. Me and Jez both shrug, and Amy delves into her handbag, which is the size of a backpack. I was a little surprised, and distinctly impressed, when out came three cans of McEwan's Export.
"Nice one mate," exclaims Jez, taking one. "I'm a sucker for nostalgia."
"That must have took some finding," I say, taking the other can.
"You are not wrong. Took me days to get these. You can't get them down here just anywhere anymore. That offy on King Street though doesn't half get some odd stuff in from time to time, so I managed to get these bad boys in there."
Jez scrutinises the can. "It's in date as well. You are a genius Ames. Ooh, I'm getting all nostalgic!"
There was a time, you see, when seemingly all you could get on a train, drink-wise, was Heineken Lager and McEwan's Export. At least on the trains I travelled on. There must have been some big deal done in some smoky boardroom (you could smoke in boardrooms back then, it was that long ago) tying the train traveller down to just these two measly choices. The thing was though, you got used to this quickly enough and after a while this particular can of beer began to taste of travel, of weekends away, and the possibility of adventure. That's why I wouldn't drink it anywhere else, it didn't seem right. More recently though, the buffet cars starting filling up with all random sorts of different choices, and that feeling has been all but diluted down to nothing. The three of us have had this conversation before and Amy not only has a good memory but also a great sense of occasion. If I ever got married, she would have to be my best man. Don't know why that thought just

popped out, I ponder, as I pop the can open.
"Cheers!"
The train arrived and the journey began.

There is no buffet car on our train, and since it is the present day, and not twenty years ago, we are *definitely* the only ones drinking McEwan's Export in our carriage. Actually, looking around we are the only ones drinking at all. It is only 11.30 after all. One disapproving look and a couple of moved seats, but not too bad a reaction. It helps to have girl in your group to look less intimidating. Which just goes to show about first impressions, as there is nothing intimidating at all about Jez and myself when you actually get to know us, and, well, let's put it this way, you don't want to get on the wrong side of Amy.

I take a sip, and look out of the window. All these familiar places whizz by. I know this journey like the back of my hand, as it were. I did come this way from time to time when visiting home occasionally but it was only when Mum was ill that I really got to spend some serious hours on this train. Look, there's that shed by those three trees, same as ever. Same graffiti still there. There's that brook that stops dead in the middle of a field. In thirty seconds we'll be speeding past this station where the train never stops. I take another sip. I always felt so bad coming back this way, back into London, leaving Dad to look after Mum on his own. Rachel had troublesome teens then, and problems of her own, so really struggled to be able to help much. I can't help but dwell on the state of Dad now, and that familiar feeling of dread rises again in my stomach. I take another sip, to push it back down again with beer, and sigh. This one can is not going to last the journey at this rate.
"Cheer up buddy!" Amy digs me in the ribs. Just wait and see what I've got planned for you!"

London. People upon people upon people. Everywhere you look, more faces of strangers. But not entirely strange somehow, all potentially knowable in some other life, some other universe. Look at them go, face after face of potential friends, or lovers, or enemies, Friends, lovers and enemies that I will never have. There's never anyone who you actually *do* know here, and actually want to meet, by happy accident.

Some of these people, if you care to look, are actually crying. In public. Face contorting and everything. What can it be that makes you shed real tears in a train station? Being parted from a loved one is the obvious one but I don't think that's always the case. Some faces look in worse pain than that, but there's no way of telling why. Not without asking, and no one wants that. See this one here. Has she just lost her job, or missed her train, lost her husband, or just been dumped after a crap two week relationship? Has she suffered abuse for years, or has she just ran out of texts on her monthly contract? Who knows? Either way I can't help, it's not my place to know. I want things to be better for her whatever the reason is, but the sad fact is that I can't even make my own life better. I suppose sometimes crying is the only option you have. I've been one of these guys before standing in this very station, losing my composure in public. Watching the empty platform long after Jen's train had left, momentarily not giving a damn who can see me. I can't help but wonder when I shall be joining their ranks again.

Jesus, just one can of beer, having not even left the bloody station yet, and I'm getting all melancholy already. Maybe I should live in a village after all. This happens every time I come to London now. I get empathy overload. All these stories I will never know, and never be a part of, moving back and forth before my eyes. I have to keep reminding myself that I can't fix the world. I need a magic wand. You can actually buy those here, just over there, I observe.

We are heading for the West End apparently, on foot, and via Bloomsbury, my old stomping ground. I expected to get a little nervous when I saw the old places again. The Jeremy Bentham, The Marlborough Arms, and all the student unions we used to congregate in. Too many memories there for me now. Pretty much all of them happy, but they won't do me any good at all these days. I'm not nervous though. I am…intrigued. Amy checks this map on her phone, and we back up to the doors of the Jeremy Bentham.

"Didn't see that there," she says. "This was first on my list. We can't go more than twenty minutes without a stop. Those are the rules."

"You've put a bit of work into this then," says Jez, looking around fascinated, with that kid-in-a-sweet-shop kind of face. Neither of these guys go to London much. They never moved far from where they grew up, and we sort of drifted a bit when I went away, so they never visited me here. So much to do, so little time. Nothing personal. No offence. None taken.

"Of course," replies Amy. "Well Mr. Capital here bangs on about all these places often enough so it wasn't hard to put an itinerary together. I've put them in this app. 'Pub Crawl' it's called."

"An app?" I ask, craning round to look. She pulls her phone away.

"Naughty, naughty. This is supposed to be a surprise."

"Has TV taught you nothing? How many surprise parties in soaps go well?" I ask.

"This is not a soap. I have written this day myself and it *is* going to go well. Don't worry, it's not all a nostalgia trip for you. Me and Jez got a vote on a couple of interesting looking places."

"Did we..?" begins Jez.

"Interesting looking places..." I begin. "...hey, what do you mean 'Mr. Capital'? Is that what you call me?"

Jez turns his gaze to Amy, then back to me. "Well, mate, when you came back for Christmas, Easter and Michaelmas or whatever you were a bit, er, full of your London experience. I mean, it was interesting to hear about it for a while but, hey, you know?"

He raises his arms to the sky. It's ok, I do know.

"Ah. Sorry mate. It *was* exciting though. Time of my bloody life." I look around at the traffic and the people and sigh. "I don't suppose it was really London I was all excited about, looking back. It was the getting away to somewhere new, feeling a little more grown up. It was the whole thing, really. The whole experience."

Amy wades in. "Oh, yes, I think we all knew exactly what you were excited about. Met her a couple of times, remember? Hmm, she was cute. I saw your point." She laughs.

Jez laughs with her. "Yeah, she *was* cute. Anyway, this place is cool, man. All these people. Are we going in then?"

I stare at that old familiar door for a moment. Of course we are going in.

We end up in the Marlborough Arms afterwards too. It's by no means twenty minutes' walk away, unless you are seriously trollied, but it was on the itinerary so we were obliged to go in. I must have banged on about this place too. One of my classes used to come here on Tuesday afternoons, after our seminar. It was our little secret, sneaking out here, the six of us. It only started because we needed to vent our spleen about this idiot in the class who tried to hijack the whole seminar as his own, with a series of stupid questions. Once again, a group was formed in alliance against a common foe. He wasn't an actual foe, he was pretty harmless really I guess, but by the time we had worked that out the group was already formed and the tradition was set. We even started inviting our other friends as the year progressed and spread the secret. That didn't spoil things at all. It made them better if anything, although it was definitely still *our* event. You know, we even invited our initial foe after a while. He wasn't so bad, as it goes. Can't even remember his name now.

While Amy is at the bar, and Jez is breaking the seal, I look around the old place and reminisce about that particular group, now all scattered to wherever. Two of them got married didn't they? How did I forget that? I wonder how they are doing. No way of knowing now, we lost touch. Didn't mean to, but these things happen don't they. As I cast my eye across the room I feel that something is wrong though. The pub sort of looks the same, but sort of looks different. What is it exactly? My eyes scoot around the ceiling, the carpet, the coving, then the bar. There's a new carpet, thank God, but the rest is recognisable. But somehow still wrong. I think it's the light. Maybe the windows are bigger? Maybe someone just washed them? Maybe it's the same thing as when I see the old house I grew up in. I move on and so the things that I used to surround myself with seem to move on too. You can never go back, so they say.
"Hey, they've got Wherry! Who knew?" Amy plonks a pint down from nowhere, right in front of my face.
"Bloody hell, Amy. Oh, Nice. Home from home."
"Where's Mr. Bladder then?"
"Mr..?"
Jez sits down, also from nowhere. I need to start paying attention or my heart is not going to last out.

"I heard that." He takes a swig of the unattended pint. "Mr, Bladder indee...ooh Wherry is it?"
"Yes, it is. Who knew?"
We stay for two. Against the rules, but Amy was prepared to let that go in the circumstances. I tell them all about the Tuesday gang. Maybe you can go back after all. If you are in the right company.

We can't go back into the student unions of course, not now, so we bypass them and head down Gower Street instead. Not to worry. They all look a bit too different now anyway, so it just wouldn't be the same. I've outgrown it, or it has outgrown me, one or the other. I do cast a wistful eye back though, as we pass through. That's just how I am.
"This place is cool!" Jez says, slapping me on the back. "But that last round was ex-pens-sive! How did you afford to do anything here?"
I shake my head. "I honestly have no idea. But we did somehow, we did."
We cut across Tottenham Court Road and Oxford Street, obviously heading into Soho. We are getting dangerously close to the twenty minute deadline. I can see no pub of note within range. As we pass through Soho Square Amy grins.
"Pit stop! She says. "This place does shot cocktails. And zombies!"

I was not hearing things after all. This place, some kind of Swedish restaurant, did have an inordinate number of shot cocktails on their menu, plus a zombie, or a replica of one at least, coming out of the wall, right towards the poor person whose round it happened to be. That seems a bit unfair. The number one cocktail on the menu had large amounts of chili in it, so me and Jez had to have one of those before we could carry on down the menu. I don't know what it is about blokes, but just like we can't walk

past a ball without kicking it, we can't pass up any kind of chili challenge either, no matter how bad an idea it turns out to be. Amy rolls her eyes and opts for something altogether tastier. Five seconds later though and it's all over, bar a disturbingly rising tingle on the tongue.
"What now?" Jez asks. "That was over a bit quick. Next bar?"
He makes a good point. That was a bit quick, but that's shots for you. The great thing about beer is that there is such a lot of it in one glass. Unless you have a half, but I don't want to even talk about that. No, a pint is not something that has to be rushed. You have long enough to form a relationship with your pint, before you eventually have to admit the inevitable and move on. Therefore you can time your night or, in this case, day by how many pints you have had. For example, my usual pace is two pints per hour. 'How long have I been here?' I may ask myself. 'Two pints' I may reply and both of me knows to a reasonable degree of accuracy what that means. Two 'pph' is a reasonable speed limit for a session I think. Landlords should have speed cameras set up at bars and flash you if you go over. Ha ha.
Amy shakes her head and heads to the bar, despite me having said none of this out loud. A few moments later she turns back. "We've just got here, seems a shame to go so soon. I'll give Handsome over there a chance to chat me up first." She blows a kiss at the zombie. "Anyway, we haven't tried the other speciality yet!"
She cackles menacingly as she passes us two Garlic Beers. Yes, that's right, Garlic Beers. But we had the last laugh. They were surprisingly good. For a lager.

Our next stop is firmly in West End tourist territory. Not my old haunt really. We would perhaps come down to this part of town once in a while on special occasions, such as

Valentine's Day, when I was still trying to impress Jen, and she was still prepared to be impressed. Amy drags us into what can only be described as a trendy cocktail bar called 'Sunrise', ushering us in, just in case we try and make a run for it. You know, I may well have been in this place before, but I can't tell for sure. None of these places round here look the same now. It's not just the location that makes you nostalgic I'm realising. It *all* has to be right – the place, yes, but also the interior, the music, the drinks served at the bar, they all have to stay the same or your memories just get washed away. Amy has the whip (not *that* whip, the other whip, the beer money) so is at the bar already, before anyone else can try and serve us.

"You used to come here?" asks Jez, watching me surveying the place.

"Maybe..." I start, Jez raises his eyebrows. "...but not when it was like this," I add hurriedly. I look around. "I *may* have taken Jen here, to this building I mean, once for a meal. I think it was here. Don't rightly know, to be honest."

"Hmm. You don't talk about her much, mate. That Jen. She was the one though wasn't she?"

"I was determined not to think that was the case when we split up," I say. "I tried to look at it as an opportunity to improve myself further."

"And how did that go then?"

"Well," I say, doing a twirl, "just look at me!"

"Onwards and upwards!" Jez offers.

Amy appears with three glasses of something best left unsaid. She hands them out and lifts hers.

"Whatever that was about, onwards and upwards! Cheers!"

"Cheers!"

"Cheers!"

"This one is a down-in-one one. Bottoms up!"

Oh my god, that was disgusting. But mercifully brief.

We end up talking to a lady called Irina in the next place. It was not at a Russian bar as you may expect, but a Spanish one. She herself is from Russia, in fact, but lives here now, despite her passion for Latin culture. This may seem a bit random from where you are standing but I'm sure it makes perfect sense to her. Rather than asking her about that, I let her tell me about her home while we sip on some Sangria based cocktail. She is from St. Petersburg, where, she says, even the alcoholics are well educated and clean. That's just what this country needs, I reply, a better class of drunk. She looks sternly at me to see if I am joking or not. Search me. Since I'm not entirely sure myself I shall let her decide. I am used to this. My mouth just comes out with this sort of stuff all the time, completely without my permission. Where does it all come from? It's my subconscious brain again of course. I'm going to have to read up on this stuff a bit more. You never know, it may stop me making such a tit of myself quite so often.

Anyway, Irina tips her head back and laughs so it appears that I am forgiven this time. I tell her about our home. She has never even heard of it. She lives in North London somewhere, and it turns out that we are familiar with some of the same places.
"Is it not strange to you," she asks Jez, who she mistakenly believes also used to live in London, "that there seems to be a fried chicken shop for every US state south of the Mason-Dixon line?"
Jez stares into the bottom of his glass and contemplates this for a moment. "I am not familiar with the phenomenon to which to refer," he slurs, "but I am, very, most very impressed to hear a Russian person reference the Mason-Dixon line in a Spanish bar. I *do* love this town!"
I assure Irina that her observation was indeed a good one, although I could not personally vouch for the Carolinas. No

matter, she says, I can vouch for both of them for you. I'm not sure what Amy is making of any of this, she mainly just watches and listens. Perhaps she just has nothing to say at this point. She's good like that. Anyway, Irina was fun and, since she seemed to take a shine to Jez, stays for a while until her friends turn up. Then she is whisked away to wherever. We all enthusiastically wave her goodbye. There she goes. We knew her for less than an hour and the meeting had no consequence whatsoever. But meeting her was better than not meeting her, so that was another little victory.

"We have one last stop," announces Amy, looking at her watch. "It may be cultural, but it is *not* touristy!"
And off we trot. Well, it is more of an amble really, at this stage, if not a stagger, but before long we end up on Broadwick Street, deep into Soho. It is not far from what I hear is the fashionable Carnaby Street, but I'm no expert on such matters. Instead of going into the promising looking John Snow pub, we are looking at a plaque on a water pump.
"I have a question…" begins Jez, holding up his hand like a schoolboy.
"Don't worry," interrupts Amy, heading off the obvious query at the pass, as it were. "We *will* be going into the John Snow. But not before we find out a little bit about him. This is the one bit of culture we are going to get today. Just the one bit, promise."
So we read the plaque. This water pump, it seems, was the source of a cholera outbreak in 1854. Dr John Snow used his noggin, and statistics, to determine that this pump was, in fact, causing all the problems, rather than nastiness in the ether, or whatever. The pump, as it turned out, was remarkably near a cesspool, but no one knew at the time that this was a particularly ill-advised piece of town

planning. Dr Snow closed down the pump and the outbreak soon ended. Hurrah.

I say, "I wonder if we are doing something equally monumentally stupid now without realising. You know, something for which we would be a laughed at by future generations reading plaques."

"Global warming?" suggests Jez, absent-mindedly.

"Ah, yes. You've got it in one. That completes my current muse. Thank you for listening."

"Seems that this is not the real pump," says Jez, still reading.

"It's a replica. That doesn't matter, Jez. It keeps the idea alive, which is the main point," I tell him.

"What you might find interesting," Amy says, as we contemplate the pump, "is that the only people round here who did not get cholera were the monks in a monastery that used to be just over there, and those others who worked there. But it wasn't God who saved them, oh no."

"What then?"

"It was beer."

"Beer?" Jez and I respond in unison.

"Beer. You see, they had a brewery in the monastery and everyone there drank beer instead of water. Turns you that the beer was way healthier than that water. And the fact that they stayed healthy helped John Snow work out what the problem was."

"Hallelujah," Jez says.

"So what you are saying," I ask, "in a nutshell, is that beer saved the lives of all those good folk in the monastery?"

"That's right! Go to the top of the class and sharpen the inkwells! *Now* can you see why we are here?"

Jez nods and points to the pub dramatically. "I do! This is not a pub crawl. This is a *pilgrimage*! Now let us tarry no further and drink to the healing qualities of the ale." And with that he dramatically strides down the street and through the doors of the pub.

"I don't know what he plans on doing in there," Amy muses, turning to me with a smile. "I've still got the whip money."

We decide to stay outside for a moment to wait and see what transpires. Not before long Jez pops his head out of the door.

"You coming then?" he says, pulling an empty pocket inside out, as if to make his point.

We end up back at the station with twenty five minutes to spare, so we absolutely have to have a swift one at the station pub. Well, you do have to, don't you? We then, of course, lose track of time a little, despite there being a large departures board in the pub. So we have to neck the last of our drinks and rush down to the platform, liquid swilling around in our stomachs. And so, in this way the day has to come to a fitting end.

I take the window seat again on the train home. It's all part of the nostalgia trip for me. As the train pulls out of the station I ponder that if this had been a movie, Jen would have been there in the Bentham, or the Marlborough or, randomly, even in that cocktail bar. She would have looked over at me and smiled. It would be like the cavalry coming over the hill to save me. I would have said something clever and engaging. But she wasn't there, was she, and I never got the chance to say anything at all. Tens of thousands of others must have passed my eyes today. Tens of thousands. But not one of them was her. She may have been just yards away, around the next corner, in the bar next door, or she could have been thousands of miles away. Regardless, she wasn't there, and I never saw her. Jesus, how drunk am I?

I focus on my reflection in the window. Jez and Amy are laughing heartily at something or other. I should join in. We head back, a little tired, and more than a little drunk, in the knowledge of having had a day well spent. We may not have saved the world, but at some point today at least we wanted to save each other.

CHAPTER 10

So time moves on and Dad's starting to lose his stories. Not the old ones, not yet, but the recent stuff. It's like his brain is going back in time, the burgeoning future locked out. He does not remember our conversation by the river about photons for example. I'm left wondering if it's the case that the more stories we collect the longer it takes to lose them all. And how can you keep the best one for last? The one you take with you when you are gone. How the hell do you even know which one that should be?

He goes in and out of lucidity, but has tried his best to adapt, and so has taken to leaving me notes when he is on the ball in case he's gone again when I come round. This is mainly rather amusing or touching, like "I HAVE been to the toilet" or "Thanks, son". My favourite is "Don't forget to read my notes." Which is funny, sort of, because by then he has forgotten he has ever written them. I always check them now. Today's one read:
"If you don't do it I will."
That one I could have done without. This was not about the washing up, clearly.

So, I figure that I should tell him as many new stories as I can, to keep him topped up, as it were, to create a buffer zone for his own. This story is not one of the best I know, but they all count, so I tell him this. This week I met this man with a marvellous job, should you choose to believe it. Get this. He actually checks word search puzzles for inadvertent swear words and removes them! Without removing the actual clues, of course. I said to him that I thought there would be some algorithm for that sort of thing, but apparently computers aren't very good at the

vagaries of swear words in such a context.
"Great job then," I said.
He humfed and shrugged. "Not doing it anymore" he said.
"Whatever for?" I asked. "It sounds great!"
He shuffled a bit, took a swig of his pint and looked down.
"Let a turd through," he sighed. "Not literally. I didn't even think that would have counted! I mean, would you think that counts?"
"No," I said, "but I'm not sure I'm the target demographic for such things. What's your name?"

Ted and I start to meet a little more regularly after that. Not arranging at first, just if we happen to be both in the pub, which was often enough as it turns out. Then, later, we swap numbers. One time down the Lion I tell him about my trip to London.
"Do you still know people there then?" he asks.
"No not really, well not so much to be likely to bump into anyway. And as it turned out, no, not at all."
"So why did you go back to all those old places then? You can't be in love with the bricks."
I think he's messing with me but I provide the obvious answer anyway.
"The places bring back the memories. Of the people who used to be there. Know what I mean?" He nods and shrugs, which means precisely nothing. "Anyway, I expect I went to the places I used to like because I thought that they would still be full of like-minded individuals."
"Oh, I hate like-minded individuals," says Ted. I take a sip and give him a moment to explain himself. "Well, where are the surprises going to come from when you just talk to people like that?"
I want to agree but I don't want to appear like-minded so I just roll my eyes. That seems to do the trick. He grins and buys me a pint.

Ted will tell me some interesting stuff from time to time. Like how IQ tests were originally invented to prove how stupid people were, not how clever. This is going to need research, but I like the idea. I'm getting the feeling that I shouldn't believe everything Ted tells me. He is clearly a convincing bullshitter. I'm doubting the original word search story already, but those puzzle books don't tend to credit the team of people responsible so that particular yarn is not going to get independently verified in a hurry, one way or the other. Not that it matters too much, but I don't necessarily want to go spreading second hand bollocks around with my name on it. Still, he might just be the kind of mate I need. He's good company and great for escapism and maybe because, you never know, I might be in need of a decent liar sometime. I'm rubbish at it, all the wrong body language and everything. Too much natural guilt. Ted, on the other hand, is evidently a natural born fibber. He tells me this with a certain amount of pride.
"Our ability to discern truth is somewhat overestimated, you see," he proceeds to tell me. "For example, there's been research done on the 'illusion of truth' effect."
"By whom?" I ask.
"Them."
"Ok. I know of 'them'. Please carry on."
"I shall. Studies show that people are more likely to believe that something is true if they have heard it before, whether or not it actually is true. Even if they suspected it were not true first time they heard it. Get this, even if they don't even consciously remember hearing it in the first place."
"That's some study."
"No doubt."
"Is that why you repeat yourself a lot then?" I quip.
"Oh yes, yes it is," Ted replies in all seriousness. "And that is why politicians and religious leaders keep on saying the same thing again and again, from campaign slogans to

ancient rites…"
"Or maybe wrongs! Sorry…do continue."
"Yeah, well they'll just keep saying it until the people believe. Turns out this is easier than finding out what the truth actually is and informing someone of that just the once."
"Fascinating," I say. "I believe it is my round." When I got back I asked "So where did you get that from then?"

Turns out that Ted is a voracious reader too. But not just books, like me. He'll read anything. Papers, magazines, quarterlies, annual reports, government reports, websites, blogs, toilet wall graffiti, wherever his interest takes him.
"But the internet," I say. "Half of what you read on there is crap. And don't tell me to just read it again a few times until I believe it. Moreover…" Yes I did say 'moreover' – at a certain point in the evening my vocabulary tends to expand before it implodes again shortly afterwards.
"…Moreover, you mentioned that it says in the Gents that Don not only will do that thing for you, he will do it for free. That's not true. Probably. And I bet that isn't his actual phone number." I quickly add. "I don't actually know that for sure either. I haven't actually tried it."
"Hmm, I don't doubt that. That's why you have to check the source or corroborate."
"I'm not asking Don. That would be embarrassing."
"Indeed. Frankly it's all a lot of hard work. Most people aren't that bothered about finding out what's actually real. It's far too much effort. I have also discovered that most people can't tell the difference anyway."
"I can sometimes tell the difference. I think," I say tentatively.
"It's tricky isn't it?" Ted replies. "Best way, unless you are obsessive, is not to care too much."
"That's kind of been my default position until I started

drinking with you."
"I'm glad I'm having a positive influence."
"I never said…"
"But when you think about it," Ted interrupts, "we, I mean us as animals, can't even see most of the universe that's out there anyway. You can't see ultraviolet, but you don't miss not being able to see it. You can't smell what a dog smells but you don't miss that either."
"Considering they usually sniff other dogs arses that it probably just as well. I know what you mean though. I've been reading about dark matter recently and sub-atomic particles and all that stuff, that are almost impossible to detect. And it now looks like most of the Universe is made of dark matter and we didn't even imagine that this stuff might exist until very recently. I think we can only detect it by maths or something. Sorry, I'm out of my depth here. I haven't finished the chapter yet."
"Yeah, I know what you mean. Mind-bending stuff, that. You know, there could be a whole other civilisation standing right here…"
"In this pub?"
"Well, round here," he waves his arms around, "but made of dark matter or in another dimension. We can't see them and they can't see us but we occupy the same space."
"Hmm, maybe that's what ghosts are. Maybe there are ghosts, drinking in a ghost pub, right here."
"Well that's another story." Ted, says, nodding his head.
"I wonder if the drinks are just as expensive in the ghost pub." I muse. "If not I would nip to the other dimension when it was my round."
"Aim high, why not?"
"I bet those other dimensions have it easy. I reckon those dark matter people are having a right laugh at us with our light matter. Like we might look down on a lite beer, you know? Yucky stuff."

"You're losing me, Dan. Anyway, getting back to my point, what I'm saying is that the truth may be out there but we are never going to get it all. It's impossible, meaningless even, so don't worry about that too much. But what *I* do, is make myself aware of my own confines of experience and understand that as best I can. Everyone else seems to just take or leave it."

"I don't know, Ted, maybe it's possible to care a little *too* much?"

"You're not the obsessive type are you."

This wasn't a question. I really don't come across as such, I know. Ted carries on.

"Anyway, I don't let the challenges put me off trying to find out as much as I can about stuff. It's not necessarily perfect but it's always better than nothing. Our experience is so limited but all the more reason to make the best of it. Stay curious, that's my motto."

Curious is what he is. For a committed fabricator he sure is flying the flag of truth a bit high. I tell him as much, since my inhibitions have disappeared for the evening, to bother someone else for a change maybe. He grins and says, "Remember though, you can find big truths within lots of little lies."

"What the heck does that mean, Ted?"

"Stories, Dan. Fairy stories, soap operas, actual operas. None of it actually happened, except Red Riding Hood as it goes, but they all should tell you something about yourself that is fundamentally true, if they are told right. Pint?"

"Hell yeah. You are really going to have to explain that Red Riding Hood comment."

And so on.

I feel the increasing need to be armed for conversations such as this, so I do a little bit of research online myself. Then, a couple of weeks later counter with this.

"Say, Ted, I was curious about your arguments on whatever actual truth is, so I did a bit of research myself. I read this article saying about how our brains are split between right and left, which can act independently of each other. In fact, people, when young, can lose a whole half of their brain and lead perfectly normal lives! Anyway, so one part of the brain can make a decision, and the other part will work to justify the decision, even though it had nothing to do with it in the first place."

I give Ted no warning at all over the resumption of this subject, since I have learned that Ted can always carry on a topic of conversation, no matter what the separation between sentences in time and space happens to be. I suspect he could manage gaps of years if necessary. It's like the experience of meeting an old school friend again years later, if they are a good sort.

"So…you mean that it's like you automatically decide to do something…" Ted begins.

"Due to some subconscious bit of programming, you know, like catching a ball or riding a bike, yeah."

"…yeah, but then your conscious brain, the *you* of you lays a story on top of that to take the credit."

"You got it."

"Brilliant," says Ted.

"So it's like you can instruct the, er right brain I think, to move, due to some stimulus the left is not aware of, via the left eye maybe, whatever, and then that person will move. But if you ask him why he moved, he will give you a reason why he wanted to, like he needs to go to the bar for a pint or something. The thing is, he, you, me, we don't even know we are doing it. Our brains don't even tell us that we are lying to ourselves."

Ted, takes a thoughtful sip. "The more you look into this stuff the more amazing it is that we know what's going on at all. If indeed we do. That last technique could come in

handy though."
He gets out a pen and writes on his beermat.
"Close your, what was it, right eye?"
I do so, but say, "this won't work Ted, I'm now fully conscious of what you are doing. Besides it is your round, no matter what the beer mat says."
He tosses the beermat back on the table.
"What's the use of all this knowledge if you can't put it to good use?"
He's just joking of course. For Ted, knowledge is an end in itself. That's why I like him.

"It's not between the right and left brain where all the real fooling and fighting goes on though," Ted continues, before he even sits back down, as he brings back the drinks. Jolly Bitter, 4.1%
"Go on," I say, as I take my first sip. Nice. He's evidently been rehearsing this while he was buying the round, so it would be rude not to allow this opener to reach its full potential.
"In fact it's not really much of a fight. It's a bit one-sided really."
"Illuminate me." Sip.
He looks me in the eye. "It's your subconscious that's really in charge, you know. Your conscious hardly gets a look in when you're talking about the decision-making process."
"How so?" Sip.
"Well most of what you do is controlled by programs your conscious brain has already written. Like when you are learning something or practicing a skill. Once the program is written it goes off to the subconscious and your conscious brain can't control it anymore. It just becomes natural behaviour and you don't know you're doing it most of the time."

"Er…"
"For example. How many sips have you had out of your pint? Don't look!"
I have to think for a moment. Three maybe? "Three." I state decidedly.
"Five. Close though."
I look at the level of beer on my glass. It does look like five sips. "Blimey. I am such an expert drinker."
"You are. You actually are. So much so you don't even need to bother your conscious brain to do it."
"That gets truer as the night goes on. Five? I don't know whether I should worry or not."
"Don't worry. Humans are naturally very poor at observation. There's just too much to take in at once, so we have to filter most of it out. So we can just concentrate on the good stuff. Like…when you notice someone in the room but you did not notice them come in. Hi Roy, didn't see you there."
I look round for Roy, who I had not seen come in. I still couldn't see him anywhere. Man, all these unknown sips can sure add up. Ted taps me on the shoulder.
"Roy's not here," he informs me. "I was being theoretical."
"Oh, right. Roy owes me a pint. Never mind. Ok, I get what you mean. If I could get my conscious brain and my subconscious brain together in a room though…"
"Well, you do now…" Ted begins.
"No, no, I mean, like, figuratively. Like marriage counselling or something…"
"I used to be…"
I plough on. "…or international peace talks." I'm waving my hands about now, imagining the scene. Ted takes a drink and smiles, picturing his own version. "I'll sit them down," I say, "and do you know what I'll ask?"
"What's that then?"
"I'll turn to my subconscious and say, 'If most of the stuff I

do is all *your* fault, why are you trying to make my conscious brain feel so *guilty* all the time?'"
Then Ted laughs, head rolled back to the ceiling. "There's no answer to that," he says. Then he stops, looks at me thoughtfully and says. "At least not today."
In return I adopt a mock pomposity and say, "But today my conscious is fighting back." Sip. "My conscious is putting alcohol into my subconscious brain as we speak." Sip. "Causing it maximum befuddlement." Sip. "Take that subconscious! Have a taste of your own medicine."
"I thought we had established that your subconscious was in charge of your drinking?"
And so on.

On my way back home I'm still thinking about all this brain stuff. Using my brain. Am I that unaware of what is going on around me? Does it even matter, if everyone is in the same boat anyway? I sure can be a bad observer at times. Birthdays, for example. I can really forget a birthday. Then sometimes I'm reading a book and find that I must have been sitting in what must have been an uncomfortable position for ages, because suddenly my leg feels all achy and I have to shift around to feel alright again, and maybe do a little dance to get the circulation going. Just the act of reading must send my eyes dancing left and right at great speed. You can see this phenomenon in others if you watch them while they are reading on public transport, but you will be ignorant of your own eye movements when reading yourself. The words just seem to flow effortlessly to you.

As I turn into my street and see the moon shine through the trees I gain a brief moment of clarity. I'm thinking of all the battles and deceit going on inside all of our brains. Maybe *that* is the point of consciousness! The only reason we have it is to create all these programs to run your life and then arbitrate between them occasionally when they are in conflict. I stop for a moment to take that in, feeling somewhat pleased with myself. This is amazing. I need to tell everyone! I need to write this down! Then I realise that Mrs. Watson from number 21 is looking out the bedroom window at me and I hurry on. When I wake up the next morning I still remember all these facts, but they seem somewhat less awe-inspiring than they did last night, and I accept that I will not be changing the world today after all. Not for the first time. Turns out I actually read that idea in another book anyway.

Poor Dad. Even the healthiest brains are trying to fool us all day every day. What chance does he have with his poor brain shrinking by the day?

"Nothing bothers you. Ever! How come nothing ever bothers you?"
It is now Saturday afternoon and I admit I got a bit bored by two o'clock so gave Jez a ring. I did not specifically suggest that we go to the pub, and neither did he, but here we are, twenty minutes later, supping on our first pint. Hop Bucket, a rather good Golden Ale, at 3.8%. A session beer, since this may turn out to be a session. Nice. This is me talking by the way. Jez had a particularly rough Friday night, but, as usual, was pretty relaxed about it.
"Things bother me," he counters. "Of course things bother me. I just don't show it so much. Doesn't everyone do that?"
We pause for a sip. He continues "Everyone except you, of course."
"Yeah, yeah, heart on my sleeve, me. So, Jez, what do you remember up to then?"

We are busy reconstructing the previous evening. Jez was with me for a while last night then had headed off to a club with some of his work mates. I wasn't in the mood so just stayed here for a couple more with Ted, who also happened to be there. The thing was that at some point Jez had lost his wallet. It contained money and cards (bank, library, breakdown recovery etc.) but the only thing he was bothered about at all was this family photo he kept in there. I knew it well. It was faded and a bit battered. He had cut it to fit into the part of his wallet with the transparent window, designed for such things. He had not particularly cut it straight, and so it always made you want to tilt your head when you looked at it. On it was his Mum and Dad, Jez himself and his younger sister, Tina. Jez must have been about in his early twenties in this picture, judging by the hair, so it must have been taken while I was away in London.

Tina is dead now. She was run over by a car, must have been a few months or so after the picture was taken. You can still see a bunch of flowers tied to a lamppost every year for her down the road, at the point where the accident happened. Jez's parents still put those flowers up there, all these years later. Sometimes other flowers appear there too. I suppose once you start to do such a thing, how can you then stop? At which point is that supposed to be enough? I don't know. You see these sort of temporary memorials up all over the place if you care to look. They don't get taken down or looked after like at a cemetery, and are invariably near the roadside, so the flowers are more often than not somewhat bedraggled and the cards are soggy and faded. These upset me a little. They are such stark monuments to the crushing grief of the parents, or whoever, sadly counterpointed by the scene around them, as the rest of the world goes by, unknowing and unfeeling. Seems cruel as you watch such a scene, but such is life. I walked past

Tina's flowers myself, on the way here today, with no more than a little nod and a wistful thought.

Jez relives his movements last night, as best he can.
"I was here..."
"Yes, I know. I was here too, remember. You had your wallet then for sure. You got a round in before you left. Did you get a round in at the club?"
He thinks for a moment. "Hmm, not sure. This bucket of beers arrived somehow. All sticking out of a bath of ice cubes. I don't think we would have needed anything else necessarily. I didn't get a kebab, unusually. I therefore might have known about the missing wallet by then, in that case."
I nod approvingly. "Makes sense. Good detective skills."
"Then walked home. Then woke up. Couple of minutes later I just had that feeling something was wrong and checked my pockets. No wallet. Always keep it in the same place. Rang the club. They didn't have it. You'd hope someone would have handed it in, but there's plenty out there that wouldn't. Bummer."
"Sorry mate. I know you liked that photo."
"Yeah, I've got others though, that's cool. I'll ring round later and cancel cards and stuff."
"Yeah, you should get your bank card cancelled. Soon as possible."
"I found this tenner in the flat though, so…another?"
That question was not deserving of a response, but it got a deft nod anyway. We had another. It failed to provide any further insight into the mystery of the previous evening. An hour later, Debbie, one of the bar staff here, started her shift. She came over and handed Jez his wallet.
"Hey, Jez. You dropped this as you were carried out last night," she said.
"Carried out?" This was both of us saying this, at the same

time. I don't remember him being carried out.
"Like a Pharaoh. Then they tipped you up a bit. When you started to work the crowd a little. Well, I was mopping up the spillages…"
"Sorry," Jez interjects, hanging his head in shame like a naughty schoolboy.
"…and there was your wallet in the puddle of beer. I've rinsed it but it's still a bit stinky."
"Thanks Debbie," says Jez, as he opens the wallet. He runs a finger over the photo.
"I didn't know how to get this to you sooner," she says, "but I thought you'd be here at some point. I bet you've cancelled your cards already, right?"
"Er…no. Was just about to. Phew. That was lucky right?" He leafs through the other sections. "All here. Look, thanks a lot, Deb. Please take this." He waves a nasty looking ten pound note at her. She waves him away.
"Please, no. You're welcome. No honestly, put it away. Just buy me a drink maybe. We will accept a note even as bad as that one in this establishment. You might not be able to spend it anywhere else."
Jez looks at the tenner. It is a mess. He smiles. "Thanks Deb. My round then."
Once he returns from the bar he says, "There you go. Nothing to worry about then."
Frustratingly, the universe has proved him right once again.

CHAPTER 11

The pub. The place where your cares can be left on the doorstep. It is not unknown though, to have a few drinks, then go back outside, pick up your cares from the doorstep, bring them back in, then parade them at large in front of a bemused audience. So experience has taught me. We had one of those today. Don't worry, he's gone now. It is best to take no pleasure in these moments. There but by the grace of God go I, as the saying goes.

I have cares, you know that much. But I tend to keep these to myself, as best I can. In fact, I spend most of my time resolutely ignoring them myself, but do check in occasionally to see if they are still there. They are *always* still there. I've generally tried not to go on about myself too much, but Ted is as curious about me as he is about everything else, so he got one decent story out of me one night. It was the least I could do for him under the circumstances. I owed him a tale or two. Thinking about it now, you could even find a metaphor in this one if you wanted to, but it doesn't make it any less true so you might as well have it too.

We had this goldfish, you see. Neither of us particularly liked goldfish, nor were our lifestyles conducive to keeping a pet of any consequence anyway. All due respect to non-consequential pets, whatever they should be. We were always out you see, working our first ever jobs of consequence, studying, or out on the lash. Well, there is really no point to being in London if you aren't going to do your best to enjoy it. You have to make up for the rudeness and claustrophobia with all the fun stuff you could get up to. Like Buckingham Palace, at first, the National Portrait

Gallery, the odd show and stuff like that. Then, latterly, pub crawls down Upper Street or round Clapham Common. I had a theory that living life in the capital was like balancing an old fashioned weighing scales. Filling up one side, you have the commute, noisy neighbours, cockroaches and the like, whether you like it or not. So you have to make it your mission to fill up the other side, to tip your life in favour of the positive. Drinks after work, taking visitors down the river on a boat trip, the open-topped bus, on a good day. And living with Jen. That filled up the good side in one fell swoop for me.

We had met at university and gravitated together, after a couple of weeks, into a gang of sorts with half a dozen or so other friends. It was noteworthy that by then none of us any longer spent time with the people we happened to meet on our first day. I don't recall any conscious decision on the matter, rather we just naturally ended up with the people we were supposed have been with. No hard feelings then. It's probably just another subconscious program running. Me and Jen became good friends quite quickly. Then some months on, once she had finally decided to move on, as most do, from her 6th form boyfriend back home, we soon became an item. Part of me thought that this getting together had always been the most natural and obvious thing, destined to be, as it were. From my perspective at least. But I was a bit shy, distinctly inexperienced, and a bit of a tosser, so another part of me thought that despite all this destiny, we might never actually complete the deal and get to be together. Happily, that latter part was proved wrong.

So was the former part, in due course. I don't believe in destiny any more, in case you're asking.

Anyway, Fingers would swim round and round the bowl and I, when in one of my darker moods, could not tear my eyes away from him, uncomfortably counting the revolutions. Me counting, not him. Ha ha. It is common knowledge that goldfish only have a memory that lasts a few seconds. Like they are constantly rebooting and wiping their hard drive in order to find wonder in repetition. This always sounded like something we just wanted to believe. I read somewhere that this may not in fact be true and that certain experiments have shown that some goldfish have memories that last for months at least. How can you get a job like that anyway, testing goldfish memories? Someone has to do it I suppose. Either way, the existence of a fish sounded like torture to me, which is why the company of Fingers normally made me feel depressed. How would *I* like it in that bowl, coming across our microwave for the first time every twenty seconds? What are you without your memories, after all? You wouldn't know in theory, I suppose, since you had lost your memory, but I felt that there must be something in his head wishing for a river, or a lake, or something instead of that damn microwave. And so I could not help but imagine that Fingers was not a happy lad.

We had won Fingers at a fairground one evening, when I, despite being a little drunk, still found the determination and dexterity to throw a bull's-eye. Always trying to impress, that was my problem back then. Fat lot of good that usually did me. Isn't "bull's-eye" a gross expression by the way? Whoever made that up? Anyway, once we had the fish we couldn't just chuck it away so we ended up having to fork out on a bowl, fish food, underwater plants and, for some reason, a model pirate ship. The last one, that was Jen's idea. Myself, if I was going to be permanently surprised by my surroundings every twenty seconds, the

sight of a pirate ship baring down on me would not be my number one choice. She liked it though, so we got it. The stall just happened to have these available, for a price. And so there they all suddenly were, in our kitchen, taking up fifty percent of the available work surface. We stood together and regarded it all, wondering 'Just how did this happen then?' She cast me one of her trademark sideways glances, with slightly raised eyebrow. We both shrugged.
"Hello fish", she said. "Welcome to our humble abode."
"Fingers." I said.
"Fingers?" She looks at me, rolls her eyes for a moment, and then laughs. "Very good. Mr Fingers, welcome to our home."

When we relived that moment, much, much later on, she revealed to me that she thought that I, in naming Fingers, was referring to the fish as an alternative food source, should we run out. I was actually thinking about gold and goldfish and Goldfinger, the movie. I accepted the laugh anyway. You've got to. But this, and general paranoia, made me wonder if she usually thought of me as more gross, and less cultured, than I considered myself.

So there you go. I'm missing out big chunks I know. There's more to a relationship than meeting up, getting together, and getting a fish. But you know that as well as me, so you can fill the blanks in as you wish. All you need to know is that I was happy for a time. Then I wasn't. At least we didn't have to fight for custody of Fingers. He was gone a good while before she was.

Ted said this was one of my better stories. Shame I had to have gone through such bad times merely to entertain people these days. Ted said I could be accused of self-pity if I wasn't careful. Ted seems to be either too honest or not honest at all, I think, but keep this to myself. Instead I turn

the comment back on him.
"So what should *you* be accused of then?" I ask him instead. I watch the cogs turning and he gives me this.

"I *was* accused of something once. Properly accused. In the dock and everything."

"Crikey." This is a surprise, well, a partial one anyway, but it does not make me uncomfortable. I can tell he's a good bloke at heart, no matter what happened. Questions inevitably surface though.

"You'll be wanting to know two things," Ted continues. "If I were any kind of story teller I would keep these back for purposes of suspense. But you want to know *now* don't you?"

I just shrugged my shoulders but in a fairly positive way and smiled at him. You *always* want to know don't you?

"Firstly," Ted states, "It was for ABH, Actual Bodily Harm." A pause. Possibly dramatic. "And no, I didn't do it." Then, "Not really."

"Some suspense then," I counter.

Ted ignores this. He's in the zone. "I was going out with this girl, see. Was around a few months at that point. It was fun mainly, didn't get too deep but we enjoyed each other's company. I don't get that too often."

"Tell me about it."

"I will. Anyway, she never wanted to spoil the mood with the details, but I did get the impression there was some bad boyfriend tucked away in her recent experience somewhere. Like she would be comparing me, favourably I mean, to some nebulous other force in her past. You know?"

He was sort of losing me but I normally get back on track with these things. "Oh yes, I know, mate," I assure him.

"Anyway, we had gone back to her home town for this thirtieth birthday party of one of her best mates from

school. I had been looking forward to it, as it goes. All those new people to meet and, hopefully, charm. Grist to my mill then as much as now. So, the night's going great and I'm playing the part of 'Interesting New Boyfriend' to a tee. I could see some of her friends were eyeing me up, you know, to see if I was going to be long-term material for Eleanor."
"Your girlfriend?"
"Yeah, I never said her name did I. Yeah, she's Eleanor. You could tell that some of those friends really loved her and so much wanted her to be happy."
"Bit much pressure there, mate." I offer.
"Not really, what will be will be. As long as you give it a fair go. Anyway, I was enjoying the moment and so was she, I think. You could spot the ex-boyfriends or wanted-to-be-boyfriends a mile off. Wanting to be nice to me, but only to impress her, not relaxed enough to even pretend to genuinely want to get to know me."
I wonder how anyone could hope to get to really know Ted, but I say "I think I may have been that ex or wished-I-was-the boyfriend before, in other circumstances. It's that obvious eh?"
"If you care to look. But these guys were ok. Ignore their low level tension and you are still having a good night out. Anyway, then this other bloke comes in and the atmosphere changes. Big time. Even amongst the exes and wannabies. He's dressed smart casual, bit too much gel, but there's nothing untoward from first glance. Still, I could tell something was up. There were a couple of mutterings of 'Can't believe he's turned up' and about half the conversations in our part of the room splutter to a close. Eleanor goes white and steps back. He clocks Eleanor at that point and, to be fair, looks a bit taken aback himself."
"So he comes over then?" I rather want to know what happens now.

"Oh no, a couple of the girls went over and told him to back off. Of course I still don't know what had happened between these two, or what this guy was capable of. He did back off though. Stayed in the same pub, but went round the corner. Maybe he looked over a few times but that was it. The chatter levels returned to normal and we carried on. No one filled in the gaps for me, and Eleanor recovered herself and just carried on. Fair enough I thought, if you can I can."

I'm starting to feel a little deflated and confused. "That's all very nice. But wasn't there some ABH?"

"Oh yes, yes there was," Ted laughs. "But that's not the main thing really. I went out for some money at the cash point down the street. On my own. Then someone tries to rob me or something and so I grab him and stick his head through the cashpoint screen."

My jaw drops, a little.

Ted chuckles, then continues. "Well, not literally through the screen. Those things are tough! Anyway, turns out it's this bloke from the pub. With the gel. I won't ever know whether he was trying to rob me, or avenge some honour thing, or whatever. But anyway, he did press charges. Once he came to."

"You must have been well pissed off."

"Yeah, I was, but life's always going to throw something at you, isn't it, or you're not living it right. Jury took less than an hour anyway, to get me off. It's just a tale to tell now, I don't think about it much."

"And what about Eleanor?"

"Hmm. We went out for a few more months. Was pretty good fun. Then we both started seeing someone else, sort of, and we drifted. I will still say hi if I see her now. She's married, has a kid or two."

"Lovely," I say, "but I meant what about her and this bloke. What was the story there?"

"She never said, and I figured it was none of my business. From her mates I gathered there was some kind of situation where he beat her up but it might have been worse…"
"Right." I can't help but sound a little frustrated.
"…and what good would *me* knowing have done if she didn't want to tell me? People can be too nosy sometimes. Secrets are fine by me if people want to have them."
He's right of course, but some part of me did want to know what happened there and my brain is already writing alternative endings in my head, without my permission and beyond my control. I then stop to think about this and decide not to feel so short-changed. Such is life. I like to keep my own secrets after all, as we all do.
"You alright for cash?" I ask, for want of anything better to offer.
Ted checks his pockets. "Thirty quid plus shrapnel. Should do it."
"Oh good, I wanted a quiet night. Don't want you getting into any more trouble out there."
Ted smiles, shakes his head and gets the round in.

I watch him operate at the bar, saying hello to people and smiling at the staff. They all smile back. He goes about everything in such an effortless manner. Why can't I be like that? I know how to act confident. I just wish I knew how to *be* confident.

Later, as I'm walking home, and feeling a little maudlin again, I try to think of the last conversation I had with Jen. How we had left things. It was way after we split up, and was on the phone. She must have heard on the grapevine that Mum had died and after a week or so rang me on the old home phone number. She didn't have my new mobile number so I expect she had tried my old one first. I smile a little as I imagine her apologising to some poor bloke, now using my old number, after she tells him how sorry she is that his Mum is dead.

Anyway, it was me who picked up the phone after all. Dad had really had enough of sympathy by then.
"Hello. 63582."
"Dan? Is that you? Is that you? Really. *Is it you?*"
I knew who it was straight away. I had been daydreaming about such a moment, of course, I had. But I won't tell you how the daydream ended. It's too embarrassing.
"Yeah, it's Dan….Jen."
"Yes, it's me. It's Jen. Look Dan. I heard about your Mum. I'm sooooo sorry."
"That's ok. Thank you for ringing though. We all appreciate the thought." I was just trotting out the same old line I had worn down from shiny and new to old and threadbare in a matter of days. It wasn't ok, as it goes. Things were somewhat quite the opposite of ok. But what else can you say? All these people ringing up are just trying to be nice.
"I'm sorry I never rang before. I didn't have your number and I didn't know if you'd still be home or not. Or if your Dad would not want to talk to me. Or you would not want to talk to me. Then I just thought 'Sod it, I'll ring. What's the worst that can happen?' So here I am. Ringing."
Pause. My daydreaming sessions had not been as adequate a preparation for this moment as you may have expected.
"No, it's good to hear from you. Yeah, yeah I'm still here. For a few more days. Just til everything's sorted. Dad still needs a bit of help."
"Poor George. Tell him I'm asking after him."
"I will." I won't. It never sounds sincere enough when I tell people that so-and-so was asking after them, so I just don't bother anymore. The world still turns.
"How's things?" she asked.

"It's been tough. But it's settling down already now, weirdly. Dealing with all the admin, keeping busy. Before you know it we're all settling into a new routine."
"So…where are you living now?"
"Still in London."
"Not the same flat right?"
"No, I didn't stay there long. Not far though. I think I'll knock the whole London thing on the head now and move back home. I feel that Dad is going to need me. It's no fun there anymore anyway."
"I'm sorry."
"Never mind. What about you?"
"Me?"
"Yes, where are you now?"
"Moved up to Wales. To be nearer *his* parents." She spared me the name. Always good with the little things, was Jen. Shame about the whopping big ones. "It's lovely there. Different lifestyle though. Just a bit!" She laughed nervously. Neither of us quite knew where this was going now, or how long it needed to last.
I took a sip of my tea, which I had forgotten completely for a moment. "Yeah, just a bit." I agreed. "It'll be weird coming back here too. In a different way. But it's probably the right thing to do."
"Yeah, you're probably right. Hey, is that old pub still there?"
"Which one? Take your pick."
"The…the…The Red Lion was it? Yeah that was it. We went there a few times at Christmases and summer and stuff. We had some good nights there didn't we?" There was a smile in her voice. Reluctantly, one crept to the edges of my mouth.
"Yeah, we did. We did. Yes, it's still there. Much the same. What am I saying? It's exactly the same!"
"Of course it is. Hey, do you remember when…?"

And so we lapsed into reverie for ten minutes or so, suspended out of time for a few brief moments. I'll spare you the details. Then she said she needed to go. I thanked her for ringing and we ended the call normally, I don't recall exactly how, as if we would speak to each other again soon. And we might have, really we might. But, as it transpired, we never did. That doesn't really seem like a fitting end now. But Jen knows me too well, I suppose. The thing is, I just hate saying goodbye. I'd rather just say nothing at all.

A few days after that last trip to the Lion with Ted, it is Mum's birthday. This is the day, more than any other day, when we will all go and visit her at the cemetery. We have also gone at other times of the year, such as Christmas, or the first anniversary of her death, but the anniversary of her actual birth seems like the best day to honour her memory. So, shortly after my breakfast, a Waggon Wheel and an apple if you are interested, Rachel knocks on my door. I have been sitting, literally, on the edge of my sofa, waiting for the knock, holding the apple core, which for some reason I have now parcelled up neatly into the Waggon Wheel wrapper. That would be an unpleasant surprise for someone, if I actually lived with anybody. Rachel is going to be driving me and Dad down to the cemetery. We could have walked, or got a bus, but she was driving anyway and insisted on picking us up. As I close the front door I look over and see that Dad is already in the car, sitting in the back. He looks so much smaller sitting back there, somehow.
"How is he today?" I quickly ask Rachel, as we head to the car.
"He's fine, thank God," she assures me. "We got lucky there. A bit quiet maybe, but he's, you know, normal."
I'm not sure she knows what normal is these days but I

leave that unsaid. I sit in the front seat and turn round to Dad.
"You alright, Dad? Bit early isn't it?"
"Morning Dan. Not too early for me. Why, bit hungover are you?"
"Don't get hangovers, Dad."
Rachel rolls her eyes at me and she starts up the car.

Mum wasn't buried, she was cremated, so there is no gravestone as such where we are going. This was not due to her wishes or anything. Despite the painful run up, it still all seemed to happen a bit too suddenly to think of such logistical matters back then. Denial at work there, no doubt. Anyway, Dad made the argument for cremation and we were all happy to go along with this. After all, we are going to run out of burial space at some point, aren't we? By the time me and Rachel are on our way out (all being well, a long way in the future) I doubt that we will have much choice in the matter. It will all be cremations by then, surely. It didn't make a difference to me what happened to Mum after she was gone. The point when the coffin either goes through the curtain, or is lowered into the ground, is just the worst moment of all, whichever way you do it. Even my limited experience tells me this. But it's also the low you hit so you can come up again.

So, instead of standing at a grave side, we are staring at a tree. It has grown visibly since I last saw it, but is still modest compared to some of its neighbours. All around this cemetery are trees dedicated to individuals or families. You can choose one in much the same way you might choose a burial plot. You choose the tree then either take the ashes away with you, or you can bury them next to the tree. We chose to bury them next to the tree, so I suppose there really is a bit of Mum here after all, if you are counting the carbon. You can put a plaque up there too, to serve as a focus for your visits, and allow you to find the right tree. This one just reads:

For Diane
Beloved Wife and Mother
Always in our hearts

I know, I know. Not really original is it? But hear me out. What if we'd put something else there instead, that later seemed to feel a bit overwrought, embarrassing, or just plain weird? Like some of those other suggestions I remember:

I shall but love thee better after death

Or

Home with God, which is far better

Or even, God forbid

Hasten, our blessed hour of reunion

Neither of those felt at all right at the time, and even less so now. For us at least. Each to their own, I suppose. I maybe could have penned something myself, but back then it was not the best time to make decisions on florid prose that would, after all, last here for centuries. I probably would have overdone it. Just in the way we gawp at old tombstones now, these very words here now will eventually be briefly catching the attention of some future human, as they randomly wander around this space, resting from the burning sun under what is, by now, a massive oak tree. And they may even more briefly wonder who Diane was, and whatever happened to her children and her husband. You know, I'm only guessing that this is an oak tree, I don't rightly know. But I like to think of it as an oak tree and imagine its future majesty. Anyway, as I read the plaque again, the wording still seems fine. There's nothing remotely untrue written there anyway.

Rachel speaks first.
"Are you sure you are ok, Dad?"
Dad looks up at her disapprovingly. "Yes," he whispers, loudly. "I said I'm fine." Then he takes her hand. "Sorry. I'm fine, really." A pause. "Hello Di."
"Hello Mum."
"Hi, Mum."
This is a strange ritual I know, since none of us are of a religious persuasion and not entirely convinced of the afterlife either. But standing here, like this, it seems rude not to recognise her presence, even if it is only in our hearts, with a polite hello. Dad takes a side glance at me, pointing at the tree trunk.
"Here's where her strength is now. In this part of the tree."
"Sure, Dad."
"And look at *all* the carbon atoms," he then says, raising his hand to point to the top of the tree. "Here is your Mum, travelling to the sky." I smile back at Dad and look up. Dad carries on, lowering his hand again.
"And in the autumn she will float back to the earth, to be picked up by a worm, or a squirrel perhaps. And from here she will start her journey around the world."
"Yeah, Dad," is my paltry offering in return.
Dad spreads his gaze around now. "By the time you are done, Diane, you will cover the world."
Neither myself nor Rachel quite know what to say to this. Last year he just cried and said how much he missed her. We seemed to naturally know how to deal with that, upsetting as it was. I do like what he just said though, it strikes some chord in me. But I have nothing to add. It's a lovely day.

So, with no prayers to fall back on, we stand in silence instead, waiting for the tears first to well up, then dissipate again. I end up staring at a space in the bottom half of the plaque at the bottom of the tree. We all know what those gaps are left there for. For the first time the gap is staring back at me.

Chapter 12

You know when you walk into a room and forget why you went in there? This is *me* doing this, by the way, not Dad. It must be the stress. I never even did find out what it was I came in here for. Oh well, It can't have been that important.

I am getting used to the ebb and flow of Old Dad and New Dad. In the sense that I can survive the encounters, I mean, not that I ever enjoy the visits to see New Dad. Today we are getting out the old photos. The doctor said it would be a good mental stimulus to do such things regularly. By the time I get old most of my photos will just be on a hard drive somewhere, drowned in the presence of their neighbours. Or, thinking positively instead, maybe I will have them beamed onto my ceiling in bed on rotation, or directly into my brain. Who knows? For today though, it's just dusty boxes and garishly coloured wallets packed with paper. We start with the really old ones.
"Look, that's one of the garden parties. We used to have great parties in the garden. Dancing, drinking. We had a laugh, didn't we? Remember?"
This is Dad speaking. I confess I don't recall these with too much clarity. Adult parties went over my head somewhat when I was a kid. Then, once I was a teenager, adult parties just didn't count. At all. We were solely interested in our own from then on.
"Surely, you remember? Your Mum loved them, fussing over our friends, keeping the wine glasses topped up, trying out the latest recipes. Vol au vents, hah!"
"Yeah, vol au vents. Always the vol au vents! What was all that about then?" I ask. That's not entirely fair. I seem to remember that I quite liked the vol au vents and would often take a handful of them before I sloped off to read a

book in a quieter corner. They seemed rather exotic at the time.

Dad looks at another picture. "Look at that! It always took a few drinks to get us dancing. But once we got started we just couldn't stop! Ah, good times. Just after this was taken it rained like buggery. We all had to crowd around the kitchen table. And here there's a picture of us there, all dripping wet. Ha!"

"I know, I was sitting there. Eating my vol au vents."

And sure I was. In the bottom right corner of the shot. Looking at the camera with a vol au vent shoved in my mouth. As if I was looking right back, through time, at me right now. I'm looking back at the Young Me too, but there's no real connection. I can hardly feel that this is the same me. It's not the same me, not really. I've been through a lot of life since then. Despite this, I can't think of a thing just now that I could tell Young Me that would be worth knowing, even if I could. If he could have another go he may well do better than me.

Another box and more pictures. All these memories. There's another one here I don't remember. I'm about six and wearing some bad shorts. Rather too red. And much too short. What was that all about? In the picture, Dad is wiping some mess from my face. It's either mud or chocolate. Probably mud. I would have remembered if it was chocolate. Why can't I remember any of this stuff? It's like I have a great blank between my first day of school and the age of eight. Although, it's not a total blank really. It only takes a photo, or a story and bits will come flooding back. *My* memories aren't gone, after all, they are just tucked away for safe keeping until the lock gets released. I think here we were on a trip to Barnard Castle, then we went for a walk by the river, where I unexpectedly found a puddle. It was all made better with an ice cream, Raspberry

ripple. Dad smiles at the picture for a while, then puts it back.
"When you get to my age what are *you* going to do? Who is going to look after you?" Dad's question cuts through my reverie with its poignancy and its unexpectedness.
"I'd better start being nicer to my nephews I suppose."
"Good luck with that."

I reach in randomly for another photo wallet. I find a picture of the four of us, plus Jasper the cat, around this very table. All smiles. All blissfully unaware of the future. Just as we are now, I suppose. I am about to show it to Dad but he suddenly grabs my arm.
"Where am I?"
Uh oh.
"You're at home, Dad. We are in this kitchen now." I hurriedly point to the picture.
He looks around. I can tell he is trying, but failing, to match the picture to our present surroundings. I pause. I have learned to allow him a little time to understand things, but also not to allow too much, in case he gets upset.
"Don't worry Dad. You're at home. You just have a bit of memory loss, that's all."
"Who says that then?"
"Never mind. Here, take a look at this picture."

Sometimes, when I look at photos, I don't think of the moment. You know, that very moment when the picture is taken. You can work stuff out from the shot itself, even if you weren't there. The looks on people's faces, how close they are to each other. How comfortable. Who is there. Who is not. What I find more intriguing is what happened just before that moment or just after, something that, unless you were there, you could never guess. Like I said, photos are a great way of jogging the memory and letting the rest of that day come flooding back, in a way you could never do if you just tried to force it. Look at these. More boxes, containing more memories. Including all those memories never captured by camera, but still there in my head somewhere. Here's some. The argument me and Jen had when we both got a little too drunk after a party. Rachel bursting in on us on my birthday, on a surprise visit back from University. My shorts splitting after the bean bag race on sports day. Look here. You can't see it, but I can. There's the first time Mum fell down with a coughing fit, in the kitchen after Christmas dinner.

Dad sits down for a doze and I carry on looking through some more pictures. It is quite addictive once you get started. And there is Jasper. We do seem to have a lot of pictures of him. Perhaps this was because he was a cat and so would not be persuaded, for anyone or anything, to pose for the camera. You couldn't review and delete your shots back then so we had to just take a load of them and hope for the best. Here's one of him washing his back-end. Nice. Dad kept all of the pictures anyway it seems, even this one. It's harder to throw something real away than to delete an electronic file. Finally, I get to a good one of him, looking to the camera, or at least to the person with the camera. He seems to have this look on his face that translates as bemusement at, once again, witnessing the strange, inexplicable behaviour of his human companions. It is a good shot though, and it makes me smile. The picture is a bit faded compared to the others. This must have been the one we put up in a picture frame for a while after he died.

He had such beautiful green eyes in that picture, and in real life. I had forgotten about those eyes. They would have the habit of looking at you as if to say 'It's alright this isn't it?' By which he meant this life, this moment, just in case you had forgotten that this was true. But seeing those eyes here and now takes me back to a dark time instead, the time when we had to take him to the vets for the final time. You see, he was a big strong boy but he was not as strong as the Leukaemia that came to take him from us. From fit and healthy to weak and jaundiced in less than three months. It was all so quick, but still no easier to witness. Jasper himself took it all so well though, much better than I did, I remember. He was a happy cat, and had always lived for the joy of the moment. This policy never changed, even when he was so very sick and could hardly move anymore. I recall that he would still purr as loudly as he could when I returned home from school and gave him his favourite scratch on the head, telling him what a good boy he was.

I felt that I owed him to be there at the end. After all, he would always cuddle up to me when I was ill, as if he felt that I needed his help. Or maybe he just liked the smell of human snot and puke. I'm joking. He was my *friend*. So, when Dad put him in his cat basket for the final time, I asked if I could go too. Dad was somewhat surprised at this request, I could see it in his face. I was not the bravest son a father could ask for normally. But I also saw relief in his eyes too. This was going to be hard on him as well. So the three of us went off together in the car, Mum and Rachel waving us off from the living room window. I was in a daze during the short drive, and then in the waiting room. I kept taking deep breaths and trying to pretend that everything was ok, to help keep the tears in and preserve my dignity.

I remember the surgery room, or whatever you call it, very clearly. Oddly, I cannot recall the faces of the vet and the nurse at all, but I remember the room. Why on earth would I block the people out and remember all the rest so well? Anyway, Dad stood back and let the vet inject Jasper, but, like I said, I felt I had to be there with him. I crouched down to his level so he could see my face. He flinched just a little as the needle went in. I told him what a good boy he was and he opened his mouth in a silent mew as he kept my gaze. Then I held his paw, said random calming words and stroked his head as I watched the lights go off in his eyes. And it *was* like that, it really was. Nothing physical that I could actually describe to you had changed at all, from that moment before to the one after, but somehow everything had changed in those eyes when the switch went from on to off. And he was gone.

It was at that moment that I could hold it in no longer and I started to shudder and cry. The faceless vet and nurse stood back and gave me my moment. They must have seen this so many times before. Then Dad came over and held me really tight. He did not berate me for being soft or girly or any of that. He just held me. I swear he had a tear in his eye himself, but he held me so tightly that he wouldn't allow me to get a good look at his face. Then we drove back home in silence, and life carried on.

'You should look at some old photos together' the doctor had said. 'It will do you some good' he said. Oh well.

I still do miss my old mate Jasper, all these years later. I'm not sure how well I would be able look after him right now, if he were still here, but I could sure do with his company when I am at home. Which isn't often enough these days, and that is the only reason why I don't have a cat now. But now I am considering that maybe the reason why I'm down the pub so much is because I don't have a cat at home. You know what? I think I would like a cat that I could take to the pub with me. That would be ideal. How could I get me one of those? I revel in that strange, but beguiling, image for a minute, me and Jasper sharing a pint, enjoying the moment.

A little later and Dad's feeling a bit better. Better enough to give me a hard time anyway. He raises the issue of a care home again. I'll leave out the gaps, the tears and the surreal digressions.

"So who *should* make the decision for me to leave my home then? Who has that right? This house is where all my memories are. I don't want to leave them here. I don't even know if I can take them with me now." He calms himself a little and carries on. "I know I've been lucky really. Up until now. It's been a good life. So I don't want to leave it behind. And now they tell me I'm going to have to prove I have the 'capacity' to make my own decisions." He sighs. "Thing is I don't always have it, do I?"

"Comes and goes, Dad. You know."

"I don't even know if I'm being brave or a coward staying here. What am I, Dan?"

"I don't know Dad. I can't answer that one of myself."

"So you understand then."

I say nothing.

"Will you miss me when I'm gone?"

"Jesus, Dad. Stop being like that. Of course I will. Stop talking like that. I don't even want to think about it."

"Miss your Mum, eh?"

"We both do."

"You know what she used to say to me? Towards the end? 'I don't want to be a nuisance'. A nuisance. Like she could ever be that to me."

"What Dad. Are you asking me to say that you're not a nuisance?"

"Oh no. No, no. I *am* a nuisance alright."

"Not really. More of a pain in the arse maybe…"

He looks me in the eye, all bright and clear again for a moment. "Agreed. Let's shake on that then."

So we shake hands. And we don't let go for a long time after that.

Later, back home on the phone to Rachel I get a little wound up, I admit. "When are you next coming to help? I can't do this every day!" But what can she say? What can she do to make this any better?

I pop out for a quick one or two to improve my mood. Dark thoughts spin round and round my head. I just need to stop thinking, stop thinking stop thinking. Arrgh! Sitting at the bar, I finish my first pint and order another. Ah look, there's Ali just come in. He's not a regular but he comes in from time to time when business is slow. I know him not so much from drinking in this place, but from him taking me here, there and everywhere in his cab. He's always up for a chat, this one, be it in his car or in here. He waves and smiles a big grin at me, oblivious to my demeanour. I suppose he gets allsorts in his car all day and has to remain resolutely positive in the face of random public reaction. I could never work with the public. I would be constantly on edge, waiting for the next idiot to inevitably come along and spoil my day.
"You alright, Ali? What brings you here tonight?"
"Quiet out tonight. Not worth it, not until later. Thought I would take a break and have some time to myself."
"Have some time to yourself with me if you like."
"I shall, Dan, I shall. Many thanks."
I get Ali a drink. He doesn't drink as such, but he says that a ginger ale does the job just as well. It doesn't, I've tried, but I admire his wish to fit in as best he can.
"Thank you Daniel. We are both on the ale then!" He laughs. It's an old joke but his laugh is genuine and infectious so I can't help but join in.
"Cheers. No one out tonight then?"
"No, always quiet until Thursdays now."
"Must be nice to get out of your car."
"No, Daniel, no, I love my car, I love driving."

"Yeah, I bet you would go on a driving holiday if you could."

He grins and then tells me something about him that I never knew. He once drove a car all the way from England to Pakistan, with some friends in the 70s, when he was a young man. They had a car each and drove from six in the morning until nine at night every day for fifteen days. No sat nav and no mobile phones then of course. They only had one map between the six of them for Gods' sake.

"Did you ever get lost then?" I ask.

"Yes, yes. Just the once. It was me. I was showing off, you see. I had a nice two litre car, petrol engine."

I don't know if this is good or not but assume so from the context, nod appreciatively, and allow Ali to continue.

"So I sped off in front of the convoy for a brief moment, then get stuck in between these two lorries as we come to a turn off. I saw my friends take the right turn and I was stuck in the middle and could not move in time. I just had to follow the lorries down the road and see where it took me."

"Where did it take you then?"

"The East German border!" he laughs. "The roads were so clear. At first I thought this was great, I'll get to the end of here, find another route, turn around and catch up. As it happens no one was going down that way because no one wanted to get over the border! By the time I headed back I was so lost, no map, nothing! All I knew was that we were stopping off that night at Munich airport."

"Glad that wasn't me." I say. "What on earth did you do?"

"Well, no panic. I was young and full of confidence. You know?"

"Er, maybe..."

"So I just drove around until I saw a sign to Munich. Followed that. Then I asked a German man outside his house where the airport was. He couldn't speak English and

I can't speak German but I made hand gestures like a plane and a whooshing noise." He does this at the bar now. A couple of people take a brief interest but no more than that. Myself, I'm grinning from ear to ear at this point.

"He gets what I mean eventually, and, since he can't tell me directions, he gets in his car and beckons me to follow. He drops me off at the airport and then there I see my friends in the car park having cups of teas from their flasks. Simple! They had only just got there themselves, but were glad to see me."

"Wow, that was lucky."

"Maybe, maybe. So I shook the German man by the hand. I had nothing to give him, and there was nothing I could say so I just shook him by the hand and smiled. He smiled back, waved at us and drove away. If I could find him now I would shake him by the hand again. A lovely man! I was so sad I had nothing to give him."

"I don't know," I say, "you gave him a good story to tell. I wonder how many times he has enjoyed telling his friends about the lost Englishman on his way to the airport, in his two litre petrol whatever."

Ali sips on his ginger ale. "Sometimes you are wise, Daniel. That makes me feel good."

"So, was it all plain sailing after that to get to Pakistan?"

"Yes, not bad. In those days, Europe was difficult and Iran was easy. Very different now. We thought about doing it again but we can't get through Iran on a British passport now and getting through Europe on a Pakistan passport is just too much trouble. Ah, it's a funny world that's for sure."

"So *Iran* was ok then?"

"Oh yes, very welcoming. Some of us sold a load of jeans in Iran to help fund the trip. They couldn't get enough of denim. Funny world!"

"Hey, once you got to Pakistan you didn't drive back again,

did you?"

"No, Daniel, I'm not mad!" he laughs and slaps me on the back. "I sold the car and flew back. That was enough driving I tell you, even for me."

He pauses and his smile fades a little. "You know, Dan, telling you this now it feels like yesterday. I can see the car now, the windscreen the dashboard. I can even smell that silly pine air freshener which was overpowering in France but smelled of nothing by Turkey. Happy times, my friend, happy times." He looks down and shakes his head, the weight of the intervening years suddenly on his shoulders. That won't do. I put my hand on his arm.

"Well, thanks for telling me that, Ali. That sounds much more interesting than my holiday tales."

"No, Dan. I'm sure you have fine stories."

We chat for a little while longer then he gets a call. He has a job on so he has to go. I turn back to the bar and my pint, realising there is a smile on my face now, one that was not there before.

CHAPTER 13

I'm now sitting here, waiting for Ted, vaguely looking around the pub for him. I'm also careful to make sure that I avoid the gaze of any pub bore who happens to be here, wanting some company. Every proper pub has at least one of these, at all times. That's the rules. I can't see any likely candidates. Oh dear, maybe it's me.

Anyway, I have come to believe that there can't be that many naturally good listeners in the world. Otherwise I surely wouldn't find it so darn easy to get people to talk to me. Or at least *at* me. After all, everyone likes to talk about themselves, don't you think, so there's no shortage of the raw material. But there does seem to be a shortage of people prepared to be on the receiving end of all of this stuff. As you know, I'm happy enough just to sit there and keep taking it all in. Bring it on. Ah, look, the door opens and there is Ted. He gives me the thumbs up as he heads over to the bar.

So we are now on to pint number four and Ted is in the mood for one of his more outlandish tales. This guy is just like *that* kid at school. You know the one, the class liar. I'm sure you must have had one too. It took a month or so for the rest of our class to work out that our class liar just made everything up, but since we had never seen our parents having sex or whatever, (and still haven't thank God!) we had no reason to doubt him. But, after he inevitably got found out, we still let him tell his tales, since they were so very entertaining. I wonder what he is doing now. Politician, ha ha.

Today, Ted is, in all seriousness, being an alien abductee. He told me that once they had got him back to Planet Whatever (sorry I can't remember the name – seemed not to matter) they gave him a standard prodding, then a couple of formal interviews. Once that particular bureaucracy has been completed they completed their assessments then offered him immortality. Ted said he didn't fancy it. He told them this apparently:
"The afterlife maybe. That would at least be something *different*. But on eternity of *this*? No thanks."
He told me that the Whatevers did not seem that surprised at the knock-back. They get a lot of that, they said, from creatures all across the galaxy. And they were always getting asked if they could offer the afterlife instead, which they couldn't.
"Seriously, Ted? How drunk, or stupid do you think I am?"
He laughs. "Not enough of either, evidently," he concedes. "Nah, I saw this on tv. One of those late night shows. Thought I would try that experience on for size. It's pretty nuts, but even so I like the idea. It's a beguiling fantasy, as fantasies go. However, I admit, if you are going to lie, at least make it convincing."
"Yeah, funny how those stories never make the news," I say.
"Well, that's the conspiracy! Joking, joking. No, the poor guy must have such an empty life to be projecting this kind of wish-fulfilment."
"Careful what you wish for," I said, for some reason. It's sometimes hard to know what to say to Ted after such things.

Ted actually, or so he says, works for a removals company. Today he has been on a local job, which is why he could join me down the pub tonight, on a week day. He has been moving out the possessions of some bloke who had just died in an old people's home. The family didn't want any of his stuff apparently so the removal company just had to get rid of it all.

"There must have been something of interest in there. Some memento or something surely?" I suggested, looking down into my pint, Big Britain, 4.6%.

"You'd think," Ted replied as he took another sip. "But it must have been just too much bother for them to go through and find anything." Another sip. "Too late now anyway. It's all been burned. Much like the owner as it happens. Shame though."

"That's poor," I say, shaking my head in an admittedly over-dramatic fashion. Hey, I did say I have had four pints, and one was a Big Britain. 4.6%. "I'm sure *I* would want to keep something, in the same circumstances. There must always be something worth remembering, right?"

"Yeah, you'd think. Miserable gits."

"I mean you couldn't keep everything, I know. But could they not even keep *one* thing?" Oh dear, I'm in danger of getting stuck in the drinkers loop here. Someone change the subject please.

"Some people eh? So…what did you keep of your Mum when she passed?"

I've not known him long but he does know the basics of my life, just to help the conversation flow. There are too many minefields in people's lives to idly banter for hours on end without knowing where the worst mines are. I chuckle nervously and say "This is a bit embarrassing, but I've still got some stuff she knitted me when I was a kid. Gloves and a scarf."

"That sounds cool. So why the embarrassment?"

"Well, ah… do I have to tell you?" I check.

"You do now…"

"Ok, it's just that they still fit me. I mustn't have grown much after she made me them. I've still got the gloves in

my coat pocket now. I hate clothes shopping you see." I show him the gloves. He eyes them suspiciously then finally with approval.
"Hmm yes, the extent of this particular shopping aversion has now been illuminated fully. Hey, you've not got your name still sewn into them have you?"
"Moving on!" I return the gloves to the depths of my pockets again.
"Ok, ok, but for what it's worth I like that. That's a great thing to keep. Ok then, so what would you keep of your Dad's when he's gone do you think?" Typically blunt.
"Jesus, Ted. I don't even want to think about that."
"But you have done, right? Thought about it."
"There's photos I suppose. Of places we used to go to, you know. Or tickets for events we went to see. Fridge magnets."
"All of them good decent memory repositories, Dan. Maybe not the magnets. What if you could just have one thing?"
I think for just a moment. "Hmm, maybe a ticket. I've lost mine, but I know Dad keeps all of them. I'd pick one from somewhere we went together, somewhere special," I muse, drifting away in thought momentarily. The sight of Ted's empty glass brings me back with a bump. "Another pint?" Ted says, "Keep 'em coming."

In return I pass this story of sorts onto Ted, which I had gleaned from a visitor to the pub the other night. Not a usual pub local, so Ted, I assume, does not know her. Elaine, as was her name. She lives round here now but had grown up on the Isle of Man.
"Sounds nice," I had suggested. It seemed like a safe thing to say. After all it looks like a good place on the map, and it had the advantage of not being here.
"Think again," she scoffed. "Peel, for Gods' sake. It's like

the Toxteth of the Isle of Man." I had heard of Toxteth, from way back, on the news. Deprivation and riots and such like. I don't know what it is like now. It could be a shining example of urban regeneration and renewal, but a reputation sticks on a place as much as a person, as we all find out eventually.

"Right." I said. "That puts it in perspective. Hang on."
I brought out my phone then brought up a map of the Isle of Man, to give me actual perspective. She didn't seem to mind. Some people do, believe it or not.

"There it is". Elaine leaned in and pointed to where Peel was on the screen. "The other side of the island to Douglas."

"Oh. Oh dear." That was me pretending to understand the implications of such a geographical placement. A risk, but one often worth taking.

"Oh dear indeed," she laughed. Barriers now down I proceeded to learn about Sweaty Eric, The German Ralph with the leather fetish, and Polish Arnie, who always carried a packet of chocolate digestives with him.

"You are sure it was *chocolate* digestives?" Ted asks.
"Sorry, I'm deviating." I said.
"Don't worry," he replies. "That's what we're here for."
This stopped me for a moment. I liked that. "That was an interesting chat anyway," I continued. "I liked her."
"Oh yes. I particularly like the sound of German Ralph. So, where is she now, this Elaine?"
"No idea," I said. "I mean it wasn't a date. We just ended up talking. Actually the last date she went on turned up in a Tux, she said."
"So? You could smarten up a bit, I'm sure, if you made the effort..."
"A tux on the top. Just boxers on the bottom apparently."
"Hmm. You probably can't compete with that. Did she

even like that, er, tux-top-boxer-look anyway?"
"I didn't ask."
"You didn't get her number then?"
"Your round, Ted."

Ted has been good for me. I think. He's a welcome distraction, at least, endlessly interesting and well worth staying another round for. He is just naturally curious, and I like that in a person. Curious about anything and everything. He's a good listener too. I suppose he likes to picking up stories so he can use himself later on. You never know, he might even actually care. I'm also getting accustomed to Ted and his ambivalence towards the truth. For example, now he is saying this:
"Careful out there."
"Out here?"
"Either or. You know, don't you, that our brains are trying to fool us all the time."
"This again. You mean our subconscious?" A sudden turn in the conversation, but that's par for the course with us two now. It's like we are playing competitive topic-recollection, and there is no time limitation. I must line something up to talk about a year from now and see how he likes that.
"Yeah, if you like," Ted continues. "Not like they are dishonest brains or anything, like in some brain-based horror movie or anything. It's just that they are so very busy and need to take short cuts to allow us to make any sense of our surroundings. Close your eyes."
"Why, what are you going to do?" I close them anyway. He's not the type to gob in your beer for a 'laugh'.
"Who is at the table by the door?" he asks.
"Er…er, it's, um. I don't know."
"They've been in front of you for about half an hour. But you didn't need to know so you don't process that

information. Because they are not Elaine for example."

"I might have noticed if it was her."

"Exactly. You received the light in your eyes but chose not to process the data in your brain. I bet that once you look you'll recognise them."

I open my eyes. Two old boys, regulars, are sitting there arguing nicely. "Ah yes, so they are."

"We can't possibly take in every single detail, so our brains decide what is important and just tell us about that, ignoring the rest. Then they fill in the gaps with expected data all the time instead, to make you think you're getting the whole picture. For example, try watching a light flashing once while listening to two beeps."

"What here? I'm not sure how…"

"Try it later." Ted says. "Point is that if you do that you will see two flashes. Your brain just makes easy connections so it can move on to the next thing."

"Didn't we have this conversation already?"

"We did?" asks Ted, as unsure as me.

"I think we did. Hmm, anyway, I suppose the drinking doesn't help here."

"I doubt it does. It really makes you wonder what is out there though, doesn't it. What is *really* out there? Like if you could experience it objectively. Like if an alien, with a more honest thought organ, could experience it."

Which leads me to enquire, "Why didn't you ask them when they abducted you then?"

He pauses a moment to look at me, but he was on a roll. "Didn't occur to me at the time. My human brain just wasn't quick enough, see?"

He looks at me over his glass, oblivious to the irony of him trying to prove one bizarre tale by referencing another. That may not be irony. Oh well, no time to check now, we're talking.

"Shame, missed opportunity." I say.

"No matter. All this brain dishonesty just helps us to see patterns and predict what's going to happen in advance. It's useful on the whole."
"I predict, Ted, that you will get the next round in."
"Poor pattern recognition, my friend. It's your turn."
"Just testing!"

While I am waiting at the bar, I muse about how strange it is that, of all the people we laud the most in society, it is the actors who we see as being top of the pile. They are the ones in all the magazines and newspapers. They are the ones whose political opinions everyone takes note of, more so than those of the politicians. If you need to promote your cause, get an actor. Yep, those who are most adept at lying have somehow happened to become the heroes of or society. Actors, those who can escape themselves and be somebody else. Now, there's a skill that could come in handy. The drinks arrive. Sip. Ooh, that's an odd one. Black Cat, 3.6%. Could get used to it though.

"Why do we all love actors so much?" I ask Ted, once I return. "Why don't we love farmers, or nurses, in the same way? People who actually help keep us alive, as opposed to mildly entertained?"
"That's an interesting point," returns Ted. "Did I tell you about that stint I did in Coronation Street in the eighties?"
"Oh *do* tell…"
Most of what followed was entirely preposterous, but I minded not one bit. He even keeps this particular extract from his memoirs on topic, which was somewhat impressive. This is frankly of some relief. All that previous talk about brains feels a bit too close to the bone at the moment, as it were. I have been trying not to think about all that stuff if I can help it, to tell you the truth. I just get images of Dad's brain wasting away to nothing, like a tree in winter. Week by week I can almost see the neurons

slipping away into the bloodstream or wherever they go, taking bits of Dad with them.

I've slowly begun to notice that I have taken to upping my number of visits to the pub lately. There could be any number of reasons for this. Maybe it's to avoid thinking about Dad. Maybe it's to try and manufacture another accidental meeting with Elaine. Maybe I'm thirsty. Either way, none of this is actually working. Dad's illness never leaves my thoughts, not really. Elaine never turns up again, at all. I've also taken to waking up in the middle of the night feeling a little dehydrated.

By the way, Dad has really not been behaving himself this week. Not at all. It's where I got this bruise from. But I'm not in the mood to talk about it. I'm here to try my best to forget it all for a few precious moments, to tell you the truth.

Chapter 14

There are, of course, horrible people almost everywhere. It is just that I have largely learned how to spot them in advance and avoid them almost entirely, which is why we won't be talking so much about them here. But don't worry, I'm not so naïve. I know they are here. They just do not deserve much time and space in this story, that's all. The way I see it, each day these people fail to grind you down is like a little victory. Look, there are two over there right now. Which is why I'm sitting over here.

Tonight is Band Night again, so I'm meeting Jez and Amy. I'm also meeting Ted so will be introducing him to the gang for the first time. Should be good. I'm looking forward to it. It gives me a buzz when friends I have get on with each other, and they generally do. The poster tonight:

Red Lion Music Night.
Playing tonight:
Similar Facilities
Revenge Pets

Only two bands tonight. One of them must actually have a decent sized set. On balance, I hope it's Revenge Pets.

Three pints in and we are all sitting at our usual table. Mr Hoppy is the drink of choice this evening, 4.1%. Ideal for the weekend when you're feeling frisky! Or, if you are me, just feeling jumpy. Ted arrives late but jovially introduces himself to Jez and Amy. I am relieved that he seemed to make a good first impression. With Amy I mean. It would be almost impossible to annoy Jez in such circumstances, so I wasn't ever worried about him. I tell them all about my bus journey into town the day before yesterday, a story I was saving just for this moment, to break the ice, should there be any.

"So this guy just sort of jumps out. And we were going pretty fast."

"Sort of jumps out? How can you sort of jump out?" Amy asks, keeping me on my toes.

"Well I didn't get a good view you know, and it happened quite quickly. He seemed to just rock a bit back and forwards, then just lurched into the road at the very worst moment."

"Bit pissed?" Jez enquires.

"Hang on, I'm not there yet. Ok, yeah, afterwards we could smell the alcohol on him. Anyway, the driver slams on his brakes like right away. All of us on the bus just shoot forward. I had to use all my strength..."

"Ha!" Amy points at me.

"...all my strength to stop me flipping over into the next seat. Then came the crunch. Way too soon. Way too soon. The bus was still flying along. I thought maybe we had hit a car from the noise, or at least a bike. But I looked up and saw it was just this fella, nothing else."

"Yikes," says Jez.

"He was lying there in front of the bus, and his body position just looked a bit wrong. Thought I had seen my first dead body."

"But not dead then?" Ted enquires.

"No, there was plenty blood and that, and he was totally still, but someone rushed over and checked his pulse and shouted out he was still alive. A whole crowd gathered round then. The bus driver was in a right state but you could tell there was some training or something kicking in and he made some calls and checked the guy. Then there was this nurse nearby and she took some charge while we waited for the ambulance."

"Lucky," says Amy.

"You're not wrong. As soon as that nurse arrived the driver just collapsed and sat in the kerb with his head in his hands. You could see his hands shaking. Couple of guys came up to him, said that it wasn't his fault, nothing he could do etc., you know."
"And where were you?" asks Ted.
"I was still on the bus."
"Hero," says Jez, raising his glass.
"Well, there was nothing *I* could do," I say, hastily defending myself. "We had to stay on board so the police could take some statements. Everyone said that the driver was in no way to blame, totally."
"So what happened after that then?" Jez asks.
"Well the ambulance took an age to get the guy in a stretcher, they had to protect his neck first and that, then they all went off. He was still unconscious. I checked the story out in the paper later. He is in a serious but stable condition, so I expect he might be ok in the end."
"But why did he ever do that?" Amy wonders. "Was he just so pissed up he didn't know where he was? Or was he, like, ending it all?"
"Not the way to do it though, in front of a bus. Jesus." says Jez, shaking his head.
"It never said in the papers," I say, "so I suppose we won't know for sure. I heard some bloke say that the same guy jumped in front of his car that morning, so, if that's true, that suggests he wasn't that happy."
"Or that sober," Jez offers.
"Hmm, but what about the driver?" asks Ted.
"Oh yeah, it was him I was wondering about really. He was so upset you know. You could see it in his eyes. Something had just snapped in him. He seemed so strong at first, taking charge of the scene, then once he had done what he had to do he just collapsed. Like something inside of him, I mean. Don't think he'll be driving a bus again in a hurry.

Poor bloke. He couldn't have done anything else, he really couldn't."

Ted looks me in the eye. "What did the papers say about *him* then?"

"Nothing," I reply with a shrug. "Not a thing. I don't suppose I'll ever know now."

"That's poor, journalists just leaving it like that. Like the driver's not important or something. He's the victim too. More so probably." Ted continues. "Some stories just don't get an end, do they?"

We all take a sip. I break the silence first.

"Yeah, so it's the driver I'm thinking of now. Not the fella on the road. Weird eh?"

"Not really," says Ted. "Well, good luck to him."

Another sip. Then Revenge Pets emerge, with a wild minor chord and cymbal crash, and the night moves on.

A little later and I'm slumped on a corner table, sat next to Ted. I assume Amy and Jez are still up on what passes for a dance floor here. I am taking the opportunity to wallow in self-pity. I know, I should not have accepted that whisky earlier but it seemed like a good idea at the time. As a result I am telling Ted, in a variety of ways, how difficult it is looking after Dad.

"You'll miss him when he's gone though. Don't lose sight of that," Ted advises me.

"I miss him *now*," I inform him back. "That's the worst thing. I miss him when he's right there in front of me, when the real him is not really there anymore. Jesus, even when he is something like his old self I can still feel his impending absence and I stand there staring at him and missing him! And he always just looks so sad now, even when he's, you know, at his best. He smiles when he thinks I'm watching, bless him, but he's not quick enough to even lie properly."

I know, I know, the whisky is making me a tad verbose. Ted lets me carry on for a moment, since I've built up some verbal impetus. "I just don't think we were built to feel like this. We've not evolved as animals to deal with having our loved ones so ill for so long, right there with us. Back on the African plains we would just die or get eaten as soon as we turned weak. Our brains just aren't built to deal with us hanging on and on."
Ted then said that he felt much the same when he first jumped out of a plane. With a parachute. He said his feet just couldn't work out where the ground was and for the first few jumps his brain couldn't help much either.
"You see, that just wasn't natural either, dangling in mid-air at fourteen thousand feet. It's all a bit surreal for a while. After a while, though, you get used to it."
I don't know if he's trying to make me feel better or just distract me. This anecdote is one of many from his amply stocked library of paratrooper stories. He continued to regale me with further tales of aerially-based military derring-do, but it all just washed over me tonight without sinking in. If you choose to believe this, he got up to all sorts of adventures and traumas in those years, apparently. But I can't engage with any of this in my current mood, so I just nod and say 'hmm' and 'mmm' at the right moments. I sure hope none of this is actually true, or I am being seriously disrespectful at this point.

A couple of pints later and, as I return from the Gents again, I can see Ted, Amy and Jez have all returned to our table. Ted is waving his hands around in an animated fashion. He will be in the middle of some outlandish tale no doubt. I'm not sure if I amply warned them about this sort of thing. Oh well.
"Hang on," Jez is saying. "Run that past me again." He is more than a little drunk and is making an obvious effort to

pay attention, although, equally obviously, is failing miserably.

Ted carries on, assessing his audience on-the-fly. "Er, how else can I put this? Er, right. You'd think that our brains lay down memories like a computer does? Don't you? Like writing a file to a hard drive."

"Well, I've not thought about it like that, to be honest. I expect so. I've been taking this for granted. I can see that now." says Jez, nodding. He often begins to take on a grander air, as his confidence in a situation begins to elude him. He's doing this now. Amy just listens, as do I.

"That is how we feel it works, intuitively. But we don't do it like that at all. We even form different types of memory and house them in different parts of our brain."

"Don't get it. How so?"

"The normal everyday stuff. Like this, for example."

"I may actually not remember this, sorry," Jez admits. "This conversation, I must tell you, may not get put anywhere in this head of mine. I hope there's not a test."

"No test. Anyway, normally this sort of stuff goes to the hippocampus." He points to the side of his head. The hippocampus isn't there. It's buried deep in the middle somewhere so you can't really point at it while sitting in the pub. We would have to go to hospital for a scan to see that, and I hope to God that we won't have to end up there tonight. This is not the best time for A&E, around now. Anyway, me and Ted have had this conversation before so I have already checked out a diagram on the internet to see where all the bits of the brain actually are. This is all new to poor Jez though.

"Hippocampus, right." He's hanging in there, pointing to the side of his head too.

"But the scary stuff, the traumatic stuff. Those memories sit in the amygdala too." Ted now points to the other side of his head. The amygdala is not there either, but it helps get the point across, which is surely enough for current purposes.

"Amidala." Jez points again with one hand and takes a swig of his pint with the other.

"Hmm. In the amygdala, the memories aren't written in the same way. They are not the same sort of memory."

"How so? I've only got one sort of memory. I think…"

"The amygdala memories, the traumas, they are more difficult to erase, more difficult to forget and, in the right circumstances, they can very easily pop up again whether you like it or not."

"Ah! Like PTSD, for soldiers?"

"Yes! Yes, just like that."

"Good, I know about this. You see all that in *so* many movies. Flashbacks and stuff."

"Right, right. So you get it then?"

"Yeah, I get it. Myself, I don't do trauma particularly…"

"He *is* very laid back," I confirm in Ted's ear. Jez continues, looking at his beer, swirling it around the glass.

"… but sometimes, though, sometimes… I can think of the day of my sister's accident, for no reason in particular really, and that can hit me pretty hard."

Ted is not sure what to do with this. I haven't told him about Jez's sister. Amy saves the moment.

"So… if I'm right," she says, "these trauma memories must be, like, an evolutionary advantage, right? It pays to remember the dangerous stuff, so you don't get yourself in trouble again."

Ted, turns to her, slightly relieved. "Exactly right, Amy. Things like this always get back to evolution in one way or other." Ted chinks Amy's glass in approval. "Those people with good amygdalas are better at keeping away from the lions or bears or whatever and so live to pass on their DNA."

I chip in. "I think nowadays my amygdala just serves to

remind me of my most embarrassing moments."

"Yes, times have changed," says Ted. "I doubt you get chased down by many bears or lions these days. But this phenomenon should, in theory, actually keep you away from creating embarrassing situations, yes?"

Jez snaps out of momentary reverie and laughs. Emotions turn on a sixpence after this quantity of alcohol. "You haven't known our Dan for long have you? Hey Dan, maybe you have a faulty amydodo. Is this, perhaps, why you haven't passed on your DNA yet?"

This causes more hilarity than it might have, but it is that time of the evening. Once Jez has recovered, he turns to Ted and chinks his glass.

"This is blowing my mind, Edward," he grins. "Fascinating stuff, really. No, I mean it. I cannot promise, however, that in this state I shall remember or learn a single thing! I can see why Dan drinks with you my friend. He's always trying to educate me and I always resist him!"

"Don't worry, Jez," Amy leans over and pats him on the shoulder. "These two don't really know what they are talking about." She then looks over to me and Ted. "Do you?" she asks rhetorically.

Ted looks at me and shrugs, then takes a sip of his pint. Up to me to manufacture a response then. Not easy at this stage of the evening.

"That is quite possible. That I cannot deny. But I'm pretty sure I might be right occasionally. No, not occasionally, *some* of the time!" I nod at Ted to illicit approval for a suitable retort. He just rolls his eyes and takes another sip. Amy waves her phone at us. "I can always check up on your facts on here," she threatens.

"Now, now. No need for that." I say, holding up my hands in surrender. Things were way better before phones, when you could just agree to disagree on a subject, sometimes for years.

But before Amy can carry out her threat the band starts up again, now with some covers. No one can handle new songs at this time of night. Amy listens for a moment, with a quizzical look on her face, then smiles. "Is it? It is...it *is* The Smiths!" she exclaims. "It's just like being back at the school disco. Time for another dance, boys."

"Warning, warning," I say, in a robot voice. "Traumatic memories reloading...loading complete!"

"Yeah," laughs Jez, "your dancing was terrible. Especially when you tried The Robot!" He turns to Ted, in case he had missed this prime piece of information. "His dancing was terrible. Really terrible. Especially when he tried the Robot."

"Got it," Ted assures him.

"He's got it Jez, he's got it. Move along. I shall now disprove your theory!"

We all get up and dance together anyway. For a long time. I may have attempted The Robot. I may not have disproved Jez's theory. For now though, I don't care what I look like, and no trauma can touch me.

CHAPTER 15

As the months drip away, I don't know which I prefer now, the lucid days or the gone ones. No, I don't mean this, not really, but Dad is becoming increasingly more belligerent in the moments when he is still his old self. Even so, these moments are becoming so much rarer now. I'm not making a chart or anything, but I can feel the slide happening, whether I want to follow the details or not. Today was a lucid day so it started, as they so often do now, with a level of disagreement. We were, as usual, discussing Dad's living arrangements, or as he prefers to call them, his dying arrangements. You know, he's not a particularly proud man and I would reckon that he would be content to find himself to be in a residential unit, or home. Especially if he could actually see himself as I see him. But he only remembers the good bits, and remains blissfully unaware of the bad. Like it's some other bloke who keeps falling over, or forgetting to eat. Plus he has his Plan. We are now having tea and biscuits.
"I know what you are saying," he lies. "But if you move me there are risks too. I will have more new things to remember. Or more likely forget! And I think I can handle it here a bit longer. My carers are really helping. Bozena is lovely. Very forgiving. Anyway, how are we going to run the Exit Plan from a care home?"
"I don't want to talk about that again, Dad." I insisted. "That is not an option."
"You want me to be safe, don't you? That's the most important thing isn't it?"
"Of course I do. I worry all the time as it is. I worry that you're going to forget where the biscuit tin is. I worry that you're going to break your head on the biscuit tin. I worry you are going to wander out into the road looking for the

biscuit tin and never come back."
"I'm not so obsessed about biscuits. You have too much imagination."
"And you don't have enough, Dad. It could happen. Are you not even aware when your mind is slipping away? If you start to feel a little odd can't you get somewhere safe and just stay there?"
"No, there's no warning. I'm either fine or it's black. No, it's not black. Because that would mean that is me there in the black. It's just nothing, me included, I am nothing too. When I wake up I don't know where I am sometimes or how I got there. It is disconcerting, to say the least." The way this actually happens, by the way, is that he is struggling through these sentences, and takes a few goes to say the word 'disconcerting'. Fair play though, he tries his best to carry on being his old self when he's with me.
"Disconcerting?" I reply. "It scares the hell out of me. Dad, can you please think about moving home again?"
"Not yet, not just yet. Look, me and your Mum lived a long time here. Longer than you. This place is part of me. It keeps me stronger being here. I remember more here…"
"Ok, ok. I get it. But at some point it won't be safe. At all. You know that."
"There's more to life than being safe, Daniel. I still want to live well, as best I can, while I'm still living."
I sit back and sigh. He doesn't realise we have had this conversation before. A few times.
I look around at the familiar walls, and paintings. "You know what? I sort of get it. I always felt safe here. When growing up. Even when the rest of the world was so confusing. You and Mum always made me feel safe, even in the moments when the world was scaring me. I don't know how you did that. I don't think I ever thanked you for that either, by the way."
"Hey, it was part of the job. I'm glad you felt that way.

That was back then though." A pause as he shuffles in his seat. "There's only one way I'm going to be safe from harm now," he continues. "I know I'm my own worst enemy, and I can't get away from me, either here or anywhere."
"Dad…"
"How long do we all want to live for anyway?" He's on a roll now. Best let him get on with it. "You can't just carry on forever. Don't fancy being one of these hundred year olds getting my telegram. They never seem that happy about it to me. On the telly."
He's going to be quite insistent today, I can see that. But inertia is a pretty powerful force in our family and I take comfort in the fact that, more than likely, we will just sit here for a bit longer, then end up doing nothing. And just carry on. He will win and stay living here. I will win and avoid promising to do anything stupid for him. So our secret stand-off will remain, to be challenged another day. I take another biscuit. Dad sits back and looks at me.
"Well if you won't do it. I will."
"Jesus, Dad. Stop spoiling my Garibaldi."

Since he's having a good day we decide to go for a walk. I say 'we' but it was him really. I was going to have another cuppa, and I'm finding our walks a little stressful these days. We naturally gravitate towards the High Street, and are, also naturally, regularly accosted, firstly by a chugger. Or charity sales operative, if I'm being kinder. I recognise the guy. I chatted to him last week about care for the elderly, but today he is all worked up about wildlife concern. That might sound unkind, sorry. Maybe he really is. You can be all worked up by more than one thing. Anyway, I attempt to steer Dad away, but he is already moving off under his own steam. Right into the path of a Jehovah's Witness or two. I'm too late to stop the leaflet getting shoved into his hands, but am able to remove us,

politely, from any further conversation. As we approach the bin, he reaches out, old habits kicking in. Then he stops. "What the hell," he says, and sits on a nearby bench. I sit with him. He reads the leaflet out loud.
"How do you view the future? Will our world stay the same, get worse, get better?"
"That will depend entirely from your point of view," I declare.
"Hmm. Not sure how much future I'm going to get a view of. Hmm, or of the past, even." Dad turns the page. "God will wipe out every tear from their eyes, and death will be no more, neither will mourning nor outcry nor pain anymore. The former things have passed away. Revelation 21 apparently. I don't know, maybe there's something in this."
"Excuse me?"
"Well, I don't feel the mourning or the pain when I am having an episode. Hmm, I can feel things passing away as well you know."
"I know, Dad. That doesn't really compare..."
"I don't know what they are. I just feel the gaps. That there should be more, but there isn't. And I don't feel the sadness, or the pain. I'm just numb. The former things have passed away. Yeah, that sure is right."
"Mmm..." is all I have to say.
"I know *you* can feel the pain, though. I'm sorry, son."
"Please don't apologise, Dad. I've told you before."
"And how am I supposed to know that?" He laughs. "And look. Isaiah here promises no more sickness or suffering of any kind. Hello Isaiah, I think you missed me! Ha, if he comes then you'll never get rid of me!"
"Nor you me."
"I'm joking, Dan, I'm joking. I think this is just telling me something I want to hear." He scrunches up the leaflet, and lofts it right into the middle of the bin, not even hitting the

sides. Impressive. As we pass by, I look in and notice that there's a good number of identical leaflets in there, in various states of disarray. I look back. The Jehovah's Witnesses are carrying on down the street, undeterred.

Something got us curious though, so as we wander through the town, a little aimlessly, we stop as we pass this church. Many a time we have walked past, but never stopped. This time, without a word, we go in and sit down near the back. It is C of E I think, but it looks quite ornate so it could be Catholic. I confess I do not know the salient points of difference. I could always go back outside and check the sign I suppose. Dad sits down and looks around.
"I just want to see if I feel something," he whispers, despite us being the only people here.
"Like what?" I whisper too. It's very infectious.
"I don't know. Anything. Here, or on the other side."
"Fair enough, father."
We remain silent for a couple of minutes. A strange calm, the like I have not felt for as long as I remember briefly descends over me. Then that familiar pull to move on takes me over again.
"Anything?" I ask.
Dad looks around, then up to the impressively vaulted ceiling. He sighs.
"Not a thing. Well, let's a give it another minute."
For some reason we both chuckle. Then someone comes in, the first other person here during our whole visit, so we muffle our laughter. She is an older lady, somewhat solemn looking. Perhaps that's how you are supposed to look in these places. Anyway, she looks over to see if she recognises us, then looks away quickly when she realises she doesn't. She sits down much nearer to the front than us and hangs her head. I lean over and whisper to Dad so she can't hear us. At least I hope so. It is so very quiet, with

just the background noise of the traffic faintly filtering through the walls.

"It's always old people you see going into churches isn't it?"

"Hmm? Well, I suppose so, son. It must be bucking the distribution curve age-wise at least. You know, I often wondered if I would start to come to church when I got older. You know, like there's some switch that goes off when you realise again that you are mortal after all…"

I stifle a laugh. Dad regards me quizzically, nods, then carries on.

"…not that sort of mortal, Daniel. Your mind is always in the pub, even when your body isn't, don't you think? No, I mean that I thought there must be some sort of pull to look into the possibility of the afterlife once your time starts to run out. Stands to reason. Like a kind of survival instinct. So I thought it might happen even to me, when I got old." Then he turns to me again. "But I'm old *now*, Dan."

"You're not…"

"I am. And *I'm* not going to be getting much older…"

We let that one hang for a moment. The woman coughs lightly and the sound echoes around. Dad looks around at all the stained glass windows for a few minutes, then abruptly stands up.

"No, I'm still not getting anything," he declares. "So I guess I'm never going to see the light now, am I?"

"Maybe not, Dad. But at least you tried."

I lean back and sigh. This echoes around the church and the woman looks around disapprovingly. So we take our leave, immediately feeling self-conscious and unwelcome.

It was a nice moment though, one out of the blue, and somewhat out of character. I ribbed Dad about it the next day but he did not respond. Sad, yet I know that even for me, in time, these memories too will fade, and disappear into nothing, our atoms all reallocated and doing different jobs for different creatures. The electrical impulses that make up our memories, and perhaps even our souls, going God knows where.

Later that day, as I was putting Dad to bed, he perked up a bit and was able to muse about his own death.
"Life." he said. "Life, when you look at the big picture, is just the recycling of carbon."
"Is that *all* there is?" I ask, relieved that Old Dad is back amongst us again.
"Sure. I read this…somewhere. We are all made of carbon largely. The bits that aren't water. So we all need to get carbon."
"Carbon-based lifeforms. As true in science as in science fiction. I learnt that first in science-fiction though." I actually did.
"That's right, son. You can learn a lot from science-fiction, as I always told you. Anyway, think about the cycle. Plants get carbon from the air…"
I chip in. I know he always liked me to. Now he more needs me to. "…from the carbon dioxide."
"Indeed. Then the animals eat the plants to get their carbon. Then other animals eat other animals, and so on."
"Sure, but think of all the stuff happens in between, Dad."
"Purely incidental. Soon I'm going to be just carbon again. Worms and fungi and bacteria will get me, then turn me into soil and gas and the plants will grow in the soil and use my carbon dioxide to start all over again. If you want to find meaning, then *that* is the point of all this. All this life. Just sharing around the carbon! I hope that one day my carbon will be put to better use."
Whether this was supposed to be some kind of comfort to me I have no idea. "It's being put to perfectly good use now Dad!"

He shakes his head. "I don't know. I never quite achieved anything lasting you know? I had plans and ideas. They aren't going to happen now, so it's up to my carbon atoms to head off and do something useful elsewhere. Bon Voyage fellas!"

He's making me think of his speech when we visited Mum's tree on her birthday. This conversation is in danger of creating emotional overload. I don't want to talk about all this now so I'm going to change the subject. Dad also just made me realise that I had no idea what his ambitions had been. I had never asked. I just assumed he was kind of a little lost, like me. "So what *did* you want to do Dad?" I asked.

He sighed and looked up to the ceiling. He is getting tired and drifting off a little. After a moment he says this:

"I wanted to be a scientist and invent something that would help people."

"Good, good. So what would that have been then?"

"I don't know, I don't remember. I had so many ideas that just came and went. I would have thought of something though, I really would, if I had just made different choices with my life. I wanted something people could remember me by. Something I could put my name to. Who is going to remember me now?"

"I'll remember you Dad."

"And when *you've* gone? And Rachel's gone? What then?"

He has a point, sadly. "You'd better hurry up and invent something then. Here's a pen and paper."

It's not a real pen and paper, it's just made of air and imagination, but he pretends to take it from me and starts scribbling in the air.

"This will be a great one," he says, smiling.

His hands are still holding the non-existent pen and paper when he falls asleep, a few minutes later. I hope he is fulfilling all his ambitions in his dreams now. That's all he's got now after all.

The next day was a gone one. I find him lying on the kitchen floor, bruises already formed on his arm. It takes me all afternoon to get him settled and calmed down, but at least he didn't need to go to hospital. That would have been truly dreadful. Bozena, Dad's favourite carer, arrives in due course and helps me sort him out. This is much to my relief, as she knows what she is doing, unlike me, and has the knack of calming him down when he is upset, unlike me. Then she has to go. Me and Dad just sit and watch the snooker for a while. I make some tea. After a while Bozena comes back to help get Dad to bed. In the bedroom, I notice a large handwritten notice on the bedside table. It says "Do not resuscitate." Bozena sees it but ignores it and tucks Dad in. I lean over to throw this away. I do, eventually, but I'm no longer quite sure if I have the right to. Whatever, a new one will be back by the end of the week anyway.
"How did I get so ill so quick?" Dad asks sleepily, as he begins to drop off.
Search me. "Just be more careful Dad, ok? Please try not to fall again."
"I'm always careful, Di."
"Your carer is here now for a bit if you need anything. It's Bozena. I'll be round tomorrow, ok?"
He waves goodbye.

I'm off to the pub. I deserve, it. I've not been all week. Besides, Ted won the lottery today. Ten whole quid, so the drinks are on him. Whoop de do.

I don't know if it was the extra ten pound's worth of beer or the general upset of the day, but I ended up spilling my guts to Ted tonight. Not in the regurgatative sense, you understand, but more in the way of emotional-unburdening.

I know you already know what I mean by this of course, but it is an odd phrase if you think about it. I mean, if I'd just invented the phrase 'spill my guts' I would not blame you if you plumped for the more literal option as the primary meaning. But words go where they will in the English language so it's no use fighting it. I'm digressing. Again. What I really mean to say is that everyone knows that Dad is not well, but I've kept details to a minimum. Even with Jez and Amy. I know they would be so supportive and all that entails, but I just don't want to burden them with any of this. I somehow feel that if they knew everything and shared this part of my life with me, this would change the nature of our relationship forever. It would always be there, in even in the good times to come, should they return, a scar on our experience together. I don't want that. This is probably selfish behaviour on my part. They would certainly both be upset to hear this, deservedly so, but they have respected by relative silence so far and I intend to keep it that way. I want to keep them for the good times, rightly or wrongly.

No, it was to this relative stranger that I revealed all my dark secrets. Once I started I just couldn't stop. He got the whole story, right from the beginning to right now. The books, the notes, the tantrums, the hugs, digression after digression, repetition after repetition. And he just kept on listening, nodding at the right times, saying the odd encouraging word, buying me drinks. Just what I needed, as it goes. Maybe it seemed ok because I felt that I had less of a relationship to spoil with Ted. Or maybe it was because he was becoming my best friend after all. I don't know, but oh yes, he got the lot. Sorry, but much more than I've told you.

"So," Ted says eventually, once I had wound myself down steadily to some conclusion, "it sounds like you have a bit of a dilemma."

"Dilemma? That's what I don't have, Ted. I'm helpless. There's nothing I can do."

"Do you mind if I'm frank with you? I have some experience in these matters. Some other time. But you *do* have a role here. Of course you do."

"And what on earth should that be?" I ask.

"You have to be with him to make this end right. Right for him. This disease is the cruellest Dan, so very cruel. You'll see this soon enough, if you haven't seen it already. Some people don't deserve what this disease gives them."

"Oh, Jesus not you as well. I can't even think of that."

"Well, you're going to have to. No one else is going to by the sounds of it. Just like he needs you now, when the time comes he's going to need you then too."

"Need me for what though. Say it."

"To grant him the ending that is right. Whatever he thinks that is."

"I can't top my own Dad!" I whisper this last bit, which in itself causes a few people to look around at me. Never whisper in public, it's always counter-productive.

"This is not just about you. He will know what he needs at the time. And so will you. You have to be there for him at the end, whatever that may be. You know that, right?"

I look at him carefully. He's staring at me with a new seriousness. What on earth lies behind all that, I wonder. I expect I will find out in time. He carries on, not waiting for a response from me.

"It doesn't have to be messy or unpleasant. It may even be beautiful."

"Right, ok," is all I can manage in return.

"You just need do what is required of you. He's your Dad."

"But I'm just me. I'm no hero or anything."

Ted shakes his head. "Best not to think that way. There are no big heroes in real life, Dan, nor big villains. There's just us."

I stare at what's left of my pint. I can't look him in the eye again. I'm so scared. I'm scared that he's wrong. I'm scared that he's right. I'm scared that I can't just let this whole thing wash over me, like I do with everything else. He gently grabs me by the arm.

"Don't worry, I can help you," he says.

FIG.3

fig.3 The electron, if not observed before the observation screen, is deemed to travel through both slits at once, acting like a wave and forming a classic wave pattern on the screen

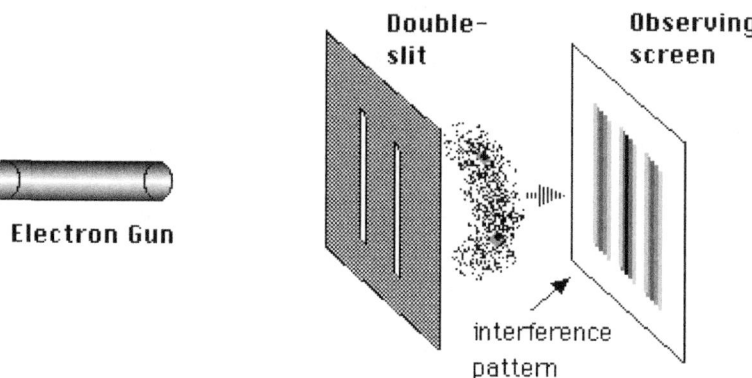

So.

I am standing outside Dad's house and I'm holding this in my hand. The key. I can feel it warming up in my palm. And so, for once, a metaphor, and an overblown one at that. Indulge me this once. I am the electron, fired at the dual slits. But I am still a wave and no one, no one can know which side I am going to come out on. As far as you know, I am in several places at once. I am guilty. I am innocent. I am irrelevant. I am in the pub. I am here. Don't worry, this is allowed in this universe. But if I am observed then this will affect everything. That's when the infinite possibilities, and the handful of probabilities, all resolve into the one actual outcome. I am.

I am a little drunk. I've really got to stop reading about Quantum Mechanics when I'm drinking.

Deep breath.

So. Now that I have removed all detectors, we shall continue in the dark.

CHAPTER 16

Who am I kidding? I can't do this. No, I *can* do this. Sigh. I can't rightly convince myself either way.

I'm just not used to these places. They are not on my radar normally. I remember visiting one when Rachel fell downstairs and broke her leg as a kid. I particularly recall Mum, Dad and I winding our way down corridor after corridor, and feeling a growing sense of both fear and fascination. All those people rushing around, dealing with someone else's vulnerabilities. There must have been thousands upon thousands of vulnerabilities all laid out within those walls that day, and every day since. Some of these would just end up as an amusing story to tell down the pub, to entertain the fellow drinkers who had just asked where you had disappeared to last weekend. Others would be the final story of all.

I doubt I quite felt any of these thoughts at the time. My main emotion was probably mild amusement that Rachel had ended up here. Plus a little annoyance that I couldn't go out and play that afternoon, as we had to visit her in hospital. No, I think I'm overlaying my current adult thoughts onto my childhood memories again. I'm sure I wasn't quite that thoughtful as a kid, nor as familiar with pub culture. Anyway, whatever the truth is about that, I do know that I am annoyed this time. I'm just not entirely sure who at.

I'm annoyed with myself because I wasn't there when Dad fell down again, this time down the stairs. I'm annoyed at the carers, who weren't there either. I know it isn't fair to think that. They weren't even supposed to be there then, and Bozena, after all, was the one who actually found him eventually. She called the ambulance, then called me, palpably in tears. Nonetheless, the anger is there anyway and I can't magic it away through logic. I'm annoyed at Rachel, because she can't come over as much as me. I'm annoyed at Dad's neighbours, who didn't hear him calling out. And I'm annoyed at Dad. There, I said it.

"What the heck were you doing upstairs anyway?" I asked him again.
He stares back at me a little blankly for a moment. Not because he is gone, his mind is relatively fine at present by our current low standards, but most likely because there is no answer that will suffice. He looks away.
"I thought I was downstairs," he says. "I know not to go upstairs anymore. I was going in the front room, and then there they were, the stairs right in front of me." He laughs. "Then, before I know it, they were right above me!"
He looks over at me to join in the laughter, but I can't do that. I can't look at him trying to convince me to do this either, it would break my heart. Some people manage it effortlessly all their lives, but I find it hard to hold onto anger, and I'm working hard to keep a hold onto it now. I need to use it for making the right decisions ahead. We both sigh.

After a few minutes Rachel rushes in, almost overshooting Dad's bed in her haste.
"Oh there you are!" she exclaims, and rushes over to kiss Dad on the forehead. "What were you thinking..?"
"Not you as well," bemoans Dad, "does anyone want to ask me how I actually *am*?" He tries to sit up straight, as if ten extra centimetres is going to retrieve his dignity.
"Sorry, of course!" Rachel switches instantly, "Does it hurt? Dan said on the phone that it wasn't too bad."
"It's bad enough," I explain. "I just didn't want you to rush or worry too much. I didn't want you thinking he was going

somewhere, you know? He's badly bruised and fractured his arm, but otherwise he'll be ok."

"Silly Dad," Rachel says as she sits down and holds his hand. There is a pause for a few moments. This might grow to be an awkward silence so I break it before it gets the chance.

"My turn next!" I exclaim. They both look at my quizzically. "Well, I've had to visit both of you in here for falling down the stairs. So it's my turn next. Your turn to visit me…you know…"

Rachel gives me that look. The one I used to get all the time when we were growing up. "I could always push you down if you like…" She's joking of course. Now that is. Back then I wasn't so sure. She turns back to Dad.

"How long were you at the bottom of the stairs for then?"

"I don't know, I wasn't straight when it happened. An hour or so maybe?"

"Oh Dad. Poor you."

She looks at me, eyebrows raised, in search for answers. In any language, this means 'what on earth are we going to do?'

My question is:
'Why am I supposed to have all the answers?'

Dad has to get seen to by the medical team and Rachel has to go and pick up the boys, so I wander off aimlessly down the corridor on my own, to kill some time. You know what they say, if you're feeling sorry for yourself just take a look around and you're bound to find someone else worse off than you. Well, a hospital sure is the right place for that. Just look around. Here's some old woman getting angry, shouting at the staff. One of the nurses is calling security, another trying to talk her down. No family there to intervene, at least not right now. Over there. Another old geezer in bed, tied up to a machine. The metal and the plastic showing more signs of life than the skin and the bone. A woman is sat in an uncomfortable looking chair next to his bed, staring into space. At the end of the ward there are two nurses stripping a bed. There's two reasons why that bed isn't needed anymore. One happy, one sad. Take your pick, depending what mood you're in.

I end up in the canteen and have a cup of something akin to tea. It is monumentally hot, and while I wait for it to cool down I swill the liquid around in the cup absentmindedly and take a look around. The Red Lion this isn't. No one is here by choice. No one is here to have a good time. Presently, one old guy wanders in and sits at the table next to me. He is in a dressing gown so I am assuming that he is a resident. We nod at each other but neither of us says anything at first. I keep catching his eye though and eventually feel compelled to say something.

"What you in for?" I ask, immediately regretting it. I know you're not supposed to ask this question in prison apparently, but I'm not really aware of the etiquette around such things in hospitals. Thinking about it, I expect it is much the same. Oh well, it's out there now.

"Cancer. What you in for?"

"Me? I'm fine. Except for this tea. Sorry about the, er, cancer. I'm just visiting my Dad. He's had a fall. He didn't know he was upstairs." A pause. "He's got dementia, see." I don't know why I had to add that last bit. I need to get used to saying it out loud I suppose.

He purses his lips knowingly, and nods. After a brief moment he looks at his watch, gets up and squeezes my arm.

"I must be off. All the best son, you take care."

"And to you," I say as he walks off.

He turns back around and shrugs. "I'm doing the chemo.

Fingers crossed I'll be fine." He smiles, waves, then turns away.

So that's the position I am in right now, taking sympathy from a cancer victim. Maybe that's not so strange. After all, this guy believes he is going to get better. Good, I sure hope he's right. But no one believes anymore that getting better is an option for Dad, not least Dad himself. There's no chemo, there's no real hope to cling to. Just an increasingly finite number of moments to count down, until they are all gone. Of course, this is true for all of us, right from birth, but we are so very good at ignoring this fact, right until the last minute, aren't we? Like it's programmed into our DNA. Then, when the last countdown begins, we will all treat its arrival as one great big unfair surprise. As if our ending has suddenly leapt upon us, rudely unannounced. 'When did I become mortal?' we shall all cry, 'How did that happen?' I sip the last of my tea, which, inexplicably, is now cold.

You know, if that cancer patient had himself come to the canteen to find someone else worse off than him, then no doubt he is considering that mission duly accomplished right now. No problem, mate, glad to be of service. Good luck to you.

Dad will be in hospital for a few more days. I take the opportunity to take a look at my options for care homes while he is still in there. We haven't discussed this properly for a while, but I think I need to bring some facts to my arguments next time the issue gets raised. I had already spoken to social services some time ago and they have arranged an appointment for me to see the obvious choice of home, which is fairly near to my place. There are no vacancies just yet (do you even call them vacancies?) but there will be soon, I was assured by our social worker. I glumly wonder who will be providing the next free place, as I look around the communal area. The care home manager has already shown me around. Everything looks fine. A bit like student halls, but cleaner. I'm sure Dad could be happy here if he let himself, and more importantly, he would be safe. It's only a few minutes' walk from the pub so it's ideal really. Well, for me anyway. I ask the manager if I could just sit down here for a bit. Sample the atmosphere, as it were. She looks somewhat harassed and seems relieved to be able to just leave me here. We shake hands then she rushes off.

So I'm just looking around and trying to enjoy the ambience, if that's the word, when, after a few moments, I seem to catch the eye of a lady sitting near the window. Not like that. She's one of the residents. She waves to me though, so it would be rude not to say hello.
"Are you lost dear?" Yes, she actually called me dear. No problem, I've been called worse.
"No, not lost no. It is my first time here though."
"Lucky you. Who are you visiting? You're not old Arthur's son are you?" She gestures over to a bloke sitting in the corner, asleep. He doesn't even look that old.
"No, I'm just looking around homes on behalf of my Dad, in case he needs a place. '*Old* Arthur'? He looks the youngest in this room. Er, no offence."
She rocks her head back and laughs raucously. Perhaps a little too much, but hey, at that time in your life you want to make the most of whatever you can get, right?
"None taken dear, none taken. Oh no, you see, it's just that he *acts* so old, you understand?"
"I'm not sure I do. Er...incontinence?" Oh my, I have to stop talking.
She laughs again, even more so this time, if that is at all possible. Once her composure is regained, she taps her

finger to her head.

"No, I mean in *here*," she says. "He's given up. He gave up the day he came here, truth be told..."

"Oh my. That's a shame."

"Some get like that. That their life ends the day they come here. The way I prefer to see it is that this is just the next phase of my life and I've got to make the most of it. In just the same way as I have tried to do in every other part of my life. It's downhill from here maybe, but it's not over yet!" She punches me on the arm. That hurt a little more than I was expecting. She has a little life in her left yet, this one, that's for sure.

"Every day a little victory eh?" I offer.

"Well, every month maybe. I'm not that near the exit door yet!" More laughter. I join in too, albeit at a relatively reduced level of volume. It is becoming quite infectious. She continues. "I like that though. Little victories. I'll use that one." She waves her hand over to the corner. "And there is Old Arthur. Just giving himself daily defeats. Grumpy sod."

"So, does he get many visitors then?"

"No, that's why I thought you might be his son, since I didn't recognise you. I don't remember anyone coming to see him since he got here."

"Maybe that's why he's grumpy."

She sighs and pulls some papers out of her handbag. "You reap what you sow in this life. He could have a nice time here if he went with it. He could be making new friends rather than dwelling on the ones he no longer has. If he ever had any. One moment, dear." She puts on her reading glasses and starts writing on card. "You've got to look on the bright side, don't you think?"

I take a look at what she is writing. This may be a little rude but she doesn't seem the type to mind. She is writing in what appears to be a bereavement card. One on the top of a whole pile of bereavement cards.

"That's not for, er...*Arthur* is it?" I ask mischievously.

She tuts, but smiles at me. "Might as well be. No, it's for a friend of mine from the church. His wife was one of my church crowd, what's left of it. She died a few days ago."

"Hmm, sorry to hear that."

"Don't worry dear. You almost get used to it at my time of life. It still hurts, but you feel somewhat, I don't know, less unfairly singled out by fate. That's why I bought a box of these."

"A box? Like you get boxes of Christmas cards? I didn't know you could even buy bereavement cards in boxes."

"Oh yes, yes, of course you can. They always come in handy. And why not? It's not like you're going to risk giving the same one to the same person again is it?" She laughs again.

"I suppose not. I obviously haven't really thought this through." She is right though. All my bereavement cards have been bought one at a time, and years apart. At some point a box of them must just make good sense. I have a lot to learn about getting old, obviously. But all in good time.

She smiles at me. "Don't worry. Once you get there you will just feel different. It's not so bad really."

I look around again. Arthur wakes up, looks around absent-mindedly, and wanders off. We both watch him go.

"Well, I hope that when your Dad gets here, he will be in a better state than him."

"I don't know about that. That will kind of depend on what kind of day he's having. Some days he can be great. Then on the others…"

She nods knowingly and purses her lips. "There are a few round here like that. You are right, it's hard to know what sort of day you are going to get with that lot. So sorry, it must be hard on all of you. I should be thankful it's just my hips with me." She stretches her legs and moans as if to

prove her point. Then she finishes her card, completes the envelope, and adds a stamp to it from a pack of them stashed in her handbag.
"Yeah, thanks, it's not easy," I continue. "But I know it's nothing special. Nothing unusual. The more you look around the more you see it. It's like it's just everywhere once you get tuned into it." She nods again. I can see at least two people like my Dad in this room now, and that's just the obvious ones.
She picks up a few magazines from the table next to her and waves them around. "There's plenty of articles about all that in these 'time of life' magazines. Here look, there's one about brain training to stop Alzheimer's here. Load of rubbish."

I take a quick look. It seems like a dumbed down version of a book I read last month on cognitive research. It's a pretty bleak read to be honest, but there is some evidence which explains why people hold onto the idea of keeping your brain active as the great hope to combat the disease. It's not quite like that though. You can't fight it, not yet anyway. What has happened though, is that some people were found to have had rampant Alzheimer's after they had died, but they had previously displayed no symptoms of the disease before their death. It turns out that these individuals were the active-brained curious types, on the whole. This caused some curiosity in a group of scientists, who then looked into it a bit more. It seems that because these people never stopped thinking and working things out, their brains, in turn, worked out several ways of doing everything. It would be like they would write a program to store short terms memories, for example, like we all do, but rather than giving up there, they keep writing new programs to do the same thing in other parts of the brain. Not consciously, you understand, just by how they live their lives. So, the upshot is that if they lose one part of the brain that they use to perform this or that action, they don't even notice. They just use the other bit without even thinking.

That's actually how the brain is supposed to work. It's designed to be never happy and, given the chance, will keep looking for new ways to do things that you have already worked out how to do. You never know, you might find a better way of doing it, so it makes evolutionary sense I suppose. Aren't our brains so different to how we appear to be on the outside! I wonder if, by living my life the way I currently am, I am doing the right sort of things to protect me from the same fate as Dad? I do think a lot, that's true. But on the other hand, I drink a lot too. But I think a lot when I drink a lot. Anyway, I shall find out in due course no doubt. It's way too late for Dad.

"Would you like to read it?" she asks. I'm suddenly conscious I have been, while staring at the magazine, thinking to myself for quite a while. I don't think I'm going to vocalise that cognitive research theory here though. This doesn't seem the time or place. We haven't even been introduced.
"No, that's fine," I say instead. "Fascinating read it is though, I'm sure. Say, can I post your card for you?"
"No, that's fine. I'm going to hobble out. It's something I should do myself. One last act for my friend. She deserves it. You take care, and don't you worry. I'll look after your Dad if he makes it here."
I'm still sitting here, staring out the window, as I watch her plod down the driveway and disappear off down the street.

Anyway, after a couple of weeks, once he got a bit better, Dad wasn't interested in taking a look at the care home. After some meetings with doctors, social workers and the family it was agreed that he could do what he liked, so he went home. He could walk reasonably well and move around the house ok, but I could see that he was never the same after that fall. It had taken something out of him. The bruises went in time but something else inside, the bit that made him *him* was never going to recover. So, there we have it. Another one of those stages coming I think. Just when you think you've got used to the last one you get bumped along to the next. And the months of this new stage begin to painfully drip by again, obscuring the ones just gone.

CHAPTER 17

Here's something for you. Almost a year ago now, when this all started, I asked Dad to tell me what his favourite memory of all time was and I wrote it down, word for word. I felt a bit foolish at the time but it's the best thing I ever did. Every day now I come over and read it to him. I was once tempted to start to embellish the tale, maybe make the George character more of a hero or something. And add car chases etc. But there's no need for that, is there. He's hero enough for me just as he is.

This is the story of a woman called Diane and a man called George. They met and they fell in love. They were young but in those days that was no problem at all. George got a job. They got married. Diane became pregnant. (Dad now always smiles at this bit.) When the day came, George was waiting down the pub for news, as was the tradition. But it was all taking too long so he downed his pint, made his excuses and ran up to the hospital. He ignored the surprise of the midwives as he burst in and took Diane's hand. It was going to be soon now. She was strong. So strong. And after what seemed like an age a baby came out. George was still holding Diane's hand and they had to be prised apart by the midwives so they could hand the baby to Diane. George began to cry.

"Who is this George?" Dad always asks now. Although the story is always the same, my answers are different, depending on my mood:
"It's you, Dad."
Or:
"Someone I met once. He's a hero of mine."
Or:

"A great man. I hope you can meet him one day. I think you would like him."
All these answers are fine with us. Now this is all we have.

My favourite memory? Well, I have been thinking about this too, and I realise that I do often dwell on a wedding me and Jen once went to. These two newlyweds were the first of our friends to get married. The wedding was in Hertfordshire somewhere so everyone was staying the night at the same hotel where the reception was being held. It was all very exciting and we all, as a group, felt like we had grown up a little bit more that weekend. Not enough to spoil the party, you understand. As me and Jen left our hotel room that evening and headed to the bar downstairs, Jen remarked on the trays left outside hotel rooms. She liked to look at them and try and guess what sort of person was in there, and what sort of time they had been having. This made no sense to me, but the next day, when I looked at the tray we ourselves had left outside of our room, I saw the remnants of a rare and special treat for a happy young couple having a special night. A kind of memento in refuse. Two bottles of wine. Empty. One piece of toast left. Both too polite to take the last one. Unread newspaper. If I close my eyes now I can still see that tray. Clearer than I can see her face, as it goes.

The moments when Dad is Dad are so rare now. There is so much pain written on his face. Written in confusion when he is gone. In sadness when he is here. It won't be long now. But I'm not ready yet. I don't think I'm ready yet.

So, when he is 'gone', I tell him about anything that comes to mind, just to keep talking. He doesn't respond in these moments but he seems to be calmer while I am speaking. I tell him about Stan and his wife's birthday. I tell him about Koachi Gazan's sunglasses, Belgian beers, Saint Bernadette and Gareth. I tell him about Ted, Ali, and Elaine. I tell him about Jez and Amy, Chloe and Betty. I tell him about the trip to London and the nice lady he might meet at the care home. I tell him about quantum mechanics, the subconscious brain and the history of tax on beer. I tell him about everything I can think of, from the mundane to the fascinating. It doesn't matter what it is now, he won't remember, so it all counts. I do this now only in the hope to improve the moment, the here and the now.

The next day was better, the best one in about a fortnight. Here we are, back at the house, with Dad tucking into a sandwich as if nothing's happened. Cheddar and Marmite, toasted. Delicious at any age, in any situation. We are discussing our book on Quantum mechanics again, although a little half-heartedly. His mind and his mouth are working at a different pace now. The conversation didn't really go like this, but you don't want to hear the real one. It's too sad, with too many pauses, and too much struggling for sense. So I'll edit out the gaps again and create something I'm going to prefer to remember. I hope you understand.

This conversation holds an extra weight for me, since I know now that this is about the last book we will ever share together. We are discussing neutrinos again, those particles that are so small, they go right through all the gaps in matter as if it isn't there at all. There's a detector for them built under a mountain in Italy, or somewhere, so deep that only neutrinos can really get a chance to get down there, and so have a chance to be found.
"I've decided I really love the idea of the neutrino after all," he says. "Bounding around the universe, being part of its beauty, but not having to interact with any of it. Not having to make any decisions or have any expectations put upon you. Not that neutrinos feel that way, I'm not that

kind of crazy. I like the idea, that's all."
"But you couldn't do without all those interactions, Dad. 'Neutrinos' don't get to have conversations like this one."
"Not quite. They just have nothing to say for themselves that's all. But they can listen to anything they like, experience everything for what it is. They can't mess any of it up." I don't know where this is going at all, bar that we are falling dangerously into clunky metaphor. No matter, I'm grateful for any interaction at all.
"They can't fall in love either," is the best I can manage, trying to fend off where I think he is heading.
"Fair point. Fair point indeed." He changes the subject, I think. "I wonder what you are going to be like when I'm gone. What are you going to do with yourself when I'm not dragging you down any longer?"
"I don't want to think about that."
"I *want* you to think about that. You're always either in the past or in the pub."
"Two places I can be happy." I declare morosely.
"Yes, me too, when I drank, and when I could remember anything! Ha ha ha. And now it's this sandwich and you." He looks at the sandwich, then me, and smiles. "Which is not so bad. But this, even this, will be the past soon enough and so will next week and next year. You're filling up your memories, Dan, but you're not filling them up with *you*. Live each day as if it's your last. Isn't that what they say? Well I am. I've decided. You've got your own life too. And you need it back."
He's right of course, but I have nothing to add, and no grand plan to offer him. I flick the pages of the book aimlessly. He takes it off me and opens it at the page where I have left it. It's talking about Decoherence. He sighs.
"I'm not going to learn anything new anymore. That's it for me and the gathering of facts. Not one new thing is going to enter this old brain. I'll just have to work with what I

have now and what I am lucky enough to still have tomorrow. What a depressing thought, eh?"

"Some people spend their whole lives like that Dad."

"True, true." A pause. "Dan?"

"Er, yeah?" Another swift change of tone. Must keep up.

"You've been good to me. I want to say thank you."

"Have I? Have I really?"

"You have. I can't imagine what this has been like for you, but I know you have done your best."

"Hey, no problem. Payback for those nappies right."

"Hmm, I can't remember dealing with many of them myself, but that can't be conclusive these days. No, I mean it, thank you." Another pause. "But I'm done now, Daniel. I am done."

We let that hang for a moment.

"I could be trying harder," he continues, staring at the ceiling. "Everyone tells you to fight all the way. But to what end, eh? For these four walls? You have to do what is right, I keep hearing. But who's to say what is the right or the wrong thing to do?"

We let that hang too.

"Are you coming round tomorrow?" Dad asks, finally turning his gaze back to mine.

"Of course Dad, I'll see you then."

"I love you, Dan."

He never says that. I'm not going to sleep well tonight.

And with that he got tired, we exchanged a few more pleasantries, and sometime later he was gone again. From the lens of a movie camera, and some slick editing, this could have been made to look like one last monumental effort of will on his part, to stay focussed until he said his last meaningful words. Words that would serve as a bookend to our relationship. Words that I would remember forever until the day I died. Words that would provide me

with the inspiration to become a better person and even perform great acts of heroism for the remainder of my existence. It always plays that way in the movies, doesn't it? But why can't someone's' last words simply be:
'Turned out nice again.'
Or:
'Your turn to do the washing up.'
Or:
'Blimey, did you need to put quite so much Marmite in that sandwich?'
There was no heroic effort here though, this was just sheer luck. You can't will yourself past neuron degeneration. Yes, it was just sheer dumb luck that allowed us that particular exchange, but I'm glad of it nonetheless.

I read the final chapter of the quantum mechanics book out loud to him. He never got that far himself. I suppose we will all finally get to a book that we will never finish. This chapter talks about a bright potential future involving powerful quantum computers, and theories that could define the very essence of consciousness, with all the particles flying between our neurons in our brains bending the very fabric of space-time itself. These seem empty concepts to me just now. I get to the end and I put the book down. I'm feeling the rate of his decline now in my bones now though, and I'm trying to ignore the realisation that today could have held the last decent, proper chat we are ever going to have together. So, although neither me nor Dad can possibly know this, just before I go, and while Bozena is getting his bed ready, I say this:
"Bye Dad."

Time to stop ignoring myself and grow up a bit maybe, is the thought keeping me company as I walk home. Sigh. Ted told me that I probably feel like a bit-part in everyone else's life, the way I go on. He has a point. I have done this to myself, I know. I have done this to myself and here is the result. Even now I have been given a real story of my own, but I have tried to be anything but the protagonist. For so many years now I've been happy to define myself by the gaps and not the substance. I've been bouncing around trying to affect as little as possible, to go by unseen and undetected. I am that bloody neutrino. I might pass you a million times before you see me.

The pub is on the way home, sort of. It would be rude not to pop in. Thankfully, no one I know is here at the moment, bar the staff. I feel the need to be here for a while, where I feel safe, but I want to be on my own tonight. After procuring a Blonde Experience, 4.2%, a pint of that is (keep it clean), I sit at the table by the door. I don't usually sit here because of the draught, no pun intended, but I feel tonight like I might need to make a swift, quiet escape if my mood changes. There are some old photos on the wall by this table and a map of the town from about 100 or so years ago. I'm ashamed to say that I never really paid them close attention before. I do so now.

Take a look. The photos are all black and white and portray scenes in this very pub mainly, mostly taken between the wars. There are several pictures of past landlords, but the ones I like best are of the normal pub folk, raising their glasses to the camera. They seem, more often than not, to be having a raucous time. Why not? They had just won a terrible war and, as yet, had no idea that they would ever have to fight another one. I wonder who they were imagining could be possibly looking back at them now. What would they make of this particular drinker? And what would they ever make of this place now? I look around. I don't know, maybe it's not so different at its heart. Yes, there's a fruit machine and all the TV screens, but the bar is still there, the bar stools and the tables, much the same. It's still a place to come to, to meet your friends, or to meet new strangers. I wonder how many of those people in that shot would happily chat to me if I was sitting there with them back then, right at the time that the picture was taken. Or, if they could, come and sit with me now. I reckon we'd all get on just fine. Ha look, right there. At the corner of one shot is a guy slumped in his seat, looking tired and wasted, but essentially happy. He looks like he's wondering what all the fuss is about, yet to see the man with the new-fangled camera. You know, he definitely looks like he would fit right in, right here, right now. Except for the hat maybe. Cheers mate, whoever you are.

I then turn my gaze to the map. This is, in fact, a map of the pubs of the town sometime around the turn of the twentieth century. Each place on the street that is, or used to be, a pub is highlighted in black. There sure were a *lot* of pubs back then. It seemed like there was a pub every few doorways. Some of them looked really small, like someone's front room converted to a boozer, which probably was actually the case. So many have now been changed to shops or flats, or just plain knocked down. I have read somewhere recently that around thirty pubs a week are closing down at the moment. I have also read somewhere that there are around sixty thousand pubs in Britain right now, give or take. Suddenly curious, I open the calculator on my phone. Just a quick calculation…that means that in two thousand weeks there will be no pubs left at all! At current rate anyway. Actually, I didn't really need my calculator for that one, that was just plain lazy. Hang on though, I don't really know what two thousand weeks is. What is that in years? Quick calculation…hang on…so that's…two thousand divided by fifty-two. That gives you…hang on…thirty-eight and a half years give or take. Just thirty-eight and a half years left to go to the pub! The clock is ticking everyone, the clock is ticking. And just what are we all going to do then? Where the heck are we all going to meet each other?

I look at the names of all the pubs on the map which I didn't recognise. Even the tiny ones had grand names. You know, proper pub names. So you couldn't tell from just the name which ones were the DIY operations and which were the big brewery pubs. I liked that. In fact, I like all these names. They are like windows to another time. Look at them:
The Lamb and Flag
The Board Inn
The Volunteer
Tap and Spile
The Globe
The Grapes
The Fighting Cocks
The Magpie and Stump
The Crooked House
The George
The Coronation Tap
The Fox and Hounds
The Bacchus
Hope and Anchor
And on and on. All gone now.

Hmm, this pint tastes a bit funny. I need to get home and get to bed. But first:
"Rachel? Hi, sorry to ring so late. I thought it would go to voicemail."
"Tom's sick. He keeps waking up to puke, so here I am. What's up, Dan?"
I hadn't prepared myself for an actual conversation. I pause.
"Dan? What's wrong? It's not Dad is it?"

"No, no. I mean yes, it is but he's still here, you know?"
"Ok, I'll see him at the end of the week, as usual. With Tom and everything…"
"No, Rachel. Listen. He's deteriorated a lot in the last few days…"
"What? What have the doctors said?" Then shouting off mic. "Hang on Tom, just sit by the bowl!"
I wait until I can hear her breathing again down the line. "They can't do anything now. They can only keep him comfortable. But he's not comfortable. Rachel, he's given up."
"But he's a fighter…"
"Rachel. He's not a fighter. That's just something people say in circumstances like these. Only some people are fighters. Only some people. But that's not Dad really, is it?"
"What are you saying?"
"Go see him tomorrow. Go see him tomorrow morning. Say what you need to say."
"Oh God. Really? I don't…"
"Rachel…"
"Oh God, Dan! Not Dad too!"
"Rachel. It's been coming. Now it's here."
I put the phone down, then say "Sorry, sis."

So I'm lying in bed now, wide awake, thinking that I maybe could have been a little more tactful, but not sure how. Half an hour ago on the sofa I couldn't keep my eyes open but the call and the act of moving upstairs was enough to leave me in this limbo state, staring at the ceiling. I muse on the undoubtedly interesting fact that this is normally due to the change of brain wave patterns from A to B, or vice versa, but this knowledge gives me no comfort whatsoever.

I think it's because I have realised that when I wake up tomorrow, things will be different.

Chapter 18

Hello. You know, I reckon that some people drink to remember and some drink to forget. Today I'm sitting firmly in the latter camp.

Do you ever get those days where your own amygdala is your own worst enemy? It takes the bad stories, the ones you never want to remember, and makes them bubble up to the surface. The more you try and push them down the harder they push back, wave after wave. Just when you thought that they had gone for good. I've been sitting here, at the bar, trying to think some happy thoughts but they just keep morphing into demons. Not demons, I remind myself, just electrical signals, just electrons, running around my body's cells in an uncertain quantum state, following the pathways they choose. They don't half make a good impression of demons though. No wonder we used to see devils and witches everywhere. We are all full of decent approximations of them, waiting for ignorance to define them.

Here's one of those bubbles. I used to love the way Jen would leave the bathroom after a shower. No, not like that. It's that she would still be wearing a towel at that point and so, presumably in order to keep it where it was supposed to be, she had this particular way of walking. It was more of a shuffle than a gait, and would take her from the bathroom, then through the kitchen and on to the bedroom. The way that the towel was tied to her body, in such an intricate way, suggested to me that nothing was going to let that towel drop to the floor, even if you really wanted it to. Even if you ran across the house like a long jumper. But apparently not. The shuffle was always required to keep it in place. All her (female anyway) friends did the exactly same thing, I noticed. Had there been a class at school for this sort of thing? Perhaps when the boys were off playing football or something all the girls were getting towel training. I just get dressed in the bathroom. What's wrong with that?

Anyway, that's not really the thing. The thing was that we used to laugh about this shuffling whenever she left the bathroom, and I would hum an appropriate tune to accompany the performance. The theme tune to 'The Professionals' was my favourite. Bolero was one of hers. Nice? Yes. Funny? To us, anyway. But the memory taunting me today was of the first time she shuffled through the kitchen, and both of us ignored it. It was from that moment that I realised something was wrong. It could have been going that way for a while, I know I'm not necessarily the most observant of characters in this regard. But looking back, the silent towel dance was the tipping point. It was good before then. It got bad soon after. Nothing happened that day at all though. Nothing at all. Funny that.

I can't watch 'The Professionals' anymore. That never used to be a problem, but it's never bloody off the telly now. I never liked ice skating anyway, so no loss there.

Over a pint of Big Tickler, 4.6%, I start musing over the conversation I had earlier with Bozena, Dad's favourite carer. She normally doesn't have time to chat. The carers get so little time allocated for each visit, and the journey time in between, that they normally have to swoosh around Dad's house like a hurricane in reverse, creating order in their wake where there was disorder before. And then they are gone. However, the client she normally had after Dad had died a couple of days earlier, and she had not yet been allocated a new person in that time slot. She could have

rushed off but she chose to spend more time with Dad instead. He, though, was soon having a doze, so she helped me tidy up the kitchen a bit more.
"People must die on you all the time in your job." I told her. Like an idiot. As if she didn't know that already! "How do you cope with that?" I say, to quickly convert this to a question.
She just looks at me with a calm smile and shakes her head. I've had that look before.
"No, that's not how I see it. The way I see it is that once I know all those people are out there who need my help, how can I not help? How can I leave it to someone else? I do not think about how it affects me. It would affect me more if I left these people alone, knowing they were out there somewhere, unhappy."
I tend to feel inadequate at the best of times. This conversation isn't helping. But she's right. It's not about me. "That's a very kind way to live your life," is all I can say.
"It is how *to* live your life, yes?"
"Yes, yes it is," I say. And I think I mean it. I've clearly been going about things the wrong way up to this point.
"But not all people feel this," she adds picking up a tea towel. "They are not so…what is the word…*human* maybe."
"Indeed." Human can mean a lot of things though, depending on the human in question. I need to change the subject. "So how did you come all this way from Poland, to end up in this place? You're from Krakow, right?" I overheard her talking about Krakow with Dad one day.
"Yes, thank you for remembering. Yes, I have come from Krakow."
"It's very beautiful, isn't it?" I had looked up some pictures on the internet once I learned where she was from. It's much more beautiful than here, that's for sure.

"Yes, thank you. It is very beautiful. Many old places are still there. Not many cities escaped the bombing like we did. In the war. Many wars."

"Hmm," I concur. I read that too. "You must miss it. We didn't get bombed here but I must say it looks like we did most days!"

She smiles, humouring me politely. "Yes, I miss home. I miss my family most of course. But I can earn better money here. The money is not good, but it is better."

"It's a shame you have to come all this way just for the money."

"Yes, this is a shame. But I also get the chance to practice my English, see another country and different people. Nice people, like your Dad. Your father is a lovely man."

"Yeah, yes he is. Thanks. He can go on a bit though. Does he keep trying to tell you his old stories too?"

She laughs. "All the time. I don't understand most of what he says but I enjoy hearing him tell me things anyway. Just for the way his face is happy. You can see his *passion*. It is enough to understand that, I think. The telling of the story is a good thing in itself, I think. Then, when he will finally stop talking I sometimes tell him a story too, like of my home."

"Yeah, he likes listening to stories too. I tell him stuff all the time now. Stupid stuff really."

"Stupid things?"

"Yeah, just things I hear people say down the pub. Random stuff from their lives."

"People's lives are not stupid. They are amazing."

She's right. Again. "You're right, you are," I tell her. "It just doesn't always make sense, that's all I mean. Ah, it's a shame you couldn't have met Dad when he was well."

"But then he would not have needed me, yes?"

I don't know. I think we all could do with someone like Bozena.

few moments. Bar exchanging money at the bar, this is the first time we have ever touched. I stare at her hand. Then a group comes in that needs serving. She lets go and moves over to see to them with a smile. But once she's done she comes right back and we chat some more. She's a good one, Debbie, a proper person. I wonder how I never noticed that before.

She's right of course. I'm not alone. Sip. There are places I could have gone to, people I could have talked too, people who aren't Ted. But somehow I never quite wanted to reach out to them, perhaps putting it off to when the moment might feel right. And it never did. Maybe it would feel right now, here with Debbie. Sip. But no, it's probably too late for me now, isn't it? I may have made a mistake there, I *may* have made a mistake. But I suppose I shall have to live with it either way.

I'm still sitting at the bar rather than one of my usual tables, when Douglas arrives. He's always here but I don't speak to him much usually. Even by my standards he is a bit depressing. But I'm sure there's a good bloke in there somewhere. Or perhaps there just was. You'll find out the problem soon enough after he catches your attention and starts talking to you.
"Alright, Douglas?"
"Alright, Dan."
Obviously, this does not necessarily mean we are both alright. Nor does it mean we are all that interested in each other's welfare. It's just the sort of verbal dance that we all do. I'm well ahead of him today for once, as in consumption of pints, so I try for an ambitious opening.
"Good day?"
"Yeah, right. Stella please, Deb. Thanks. Got another text from *her* today."
He doesn't mean Stella. Ha ha. He means his wife, or ex-

wife. I can't remember her name. It could be Stella.
"Really? She texted *you*? What did she want?" Maybe this won't be so bad after all.
"Told me to leave her alone or she'd get an injunction."
"Ah, sorry mate." Business as usual then.
"Funny, isn't it? You could ask around this pub right now and I bet everyone here knows what an injunction is. Everyone's throwing them around these days." Douglas is just staring at his pint and hasn't even looked at me yet. He takes a mighty swig.
"Yeah, I suppose so. Celebrity stories and that I suppose."
"Go back a generation and I bet no one here would know what one was. Here's to progress eh. Let's all just put up these *walls* to keep us apart. That'll make us all happier!" One more swig. Half a pint gone already. He'll be soaring past me like an eagle within the hour at this rate.
"Where did you see her then? Down the shops?"
"Nah." Swig. "Round the house. Our house. My bloody house. I needed to pick something up."
"What was that? You got all your vinyl a while back, right?"
"Doesn't matter." Swig. "Deb? Yeah, same. Cheers. Just use this one. Ta. No, mate, she was not best pleased."
"Doug…"
"Tosser was there."
"Oh, sorry mate. What did you do?"
"Nothing. I was, like, just stunned. Not like it was a surprise, though. I know what's going on really, when I think about it. When I have to think about it. It was, like, I was thinking that *I* should have been there, not him. I just stood there wondering how the hell that had all happened. Don't know how long I was standing there for. She just started shouting at me after a while. She told him to stay away. From the garden, I mean. Thanks Deb. Here you go. Neighbours came out too, for a look. Then I couldn't even

remember why I was there."

"Doug..."

"Something clicked and then I just wanted to go. But I couldn't move my legs. I kept looking through the window at the sofa. I used to love sitting on that sofa. Watching the football. Curling up with her, even. That spot on the right was my spot. Felt at *home* there. Right there."

"Why don't you ask for the sofa back?" I said, instantly regretting my semi-drunken candour. "Sorry, I don't mean... you know. Ah, it won't be the *same*, I know, but it might be something?"

He takes another big swig. He looks over to me for the first time. Raises his eyebrows. He can tell I'm a little pissed, I think. "You might have something there, Dan, you might have something there. Would at least stop *him* planting his arse, or whatever else, on it."

"Maybe, through your solicitors though, yeah? I'm not saying, like, just go and get it."

"Of course. I'm not stupid." He sighs. "I know when I'm beat." Swig. "You know, it was like the sound went off. And all I could see was the window and the sofa. The window and the sofa. Then I felt her pushing me. Pushing me out the garden. She was mad. Really mad. I just let her push me. Once I was through the gate she stopped and went back inside. The neighbours backed away. Couldn't look me in the eye. Then they went in without a word. Ten years we lived next to them. Ten years."

"Hmm. Best leave it a while mate. You don't want to get into trouble."

"I shouldn't even *be* in trouble. I never bloody did anything... Deb?"

"I'll get these, Douglas. Yeah, same again. Thanks Debbie."

And on we went. After an hour or so he had exhausted all current avenues of self-torment and we had taken to swapping our Top Favourite Films in any-given-genre. Best rom com? Easy, there's only been one good one hasn't there? Best science fiction film? Somewhat more tricky. I don't remember if we came to any meaningful consensus on that one. That debate never gets satisfactorily concluded, in my experience. Best buddy movie? What's a bloody buddy movie, Doug asked. If I have to explain that, then I don't know how you are going to pick your favourite, I said. As it goes I think we agreed on that one eventually, whatever that was. Debbie joined in for a while when she could, which, I think, confused the debate somewhat. But there's nothing wrong with such things getting thoroughly confused in these situations, I find. It all adds to the mix.

And so, if you had looked over at us just then, halfway through the evening, you'd have seen these two guys, debating animatedly, having a good old laugh, without a care in the world. Keep that image, that snapshot, in your head why don't you. Save it for the next time you are out. Nice eh? Yeah, remember everyone looks normal from back here.

And so Doug went off. I stayed a while longer, sat at a table in the corner and read my book. Our book. I read the chapter about the dual slit experiment again. Later, the pub filled up and I shared the table with a nice couple called Jess and Adam. I even took a nice picture for them. Then I let them have the table to themselves. It was alright chatting for a while, but I was just in the way.

Forgive me.

The End

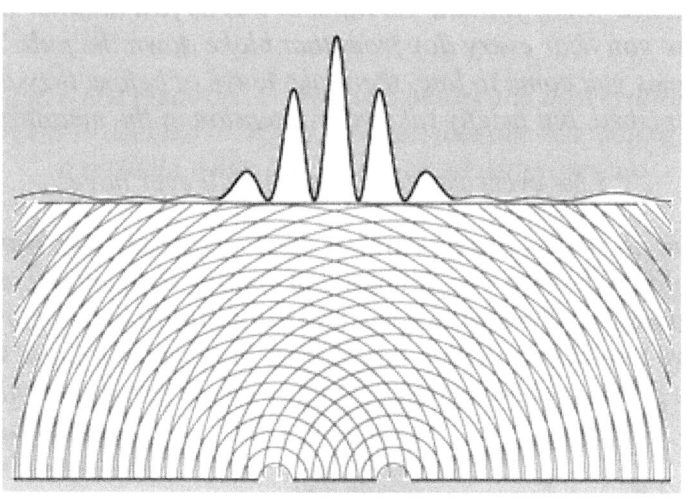

Note from the Author

Thank you for reading my book. Really. I hope you found something in it that spoke to you.

I would love to carry on writing more books and what really helps new authors more than anything can be summed up in one word.

Reviews.

The more reviews we get online the more those algorithms notice us and promote us to other readers. So if you could please take the time to write a review, such as on Amazon, that would be really helpful. Even just a few words is fine.

Reviews also let me know what is working for readers and what is not, and that is also a very good thing, as I 'sit here in the pub' with Dan, deciding what he is going to do next.

We both hope you meet you down The Red Lion again soon.

Cheers.

Mark Fryday

Sept 2015

Printed in Great Britain
by Amazon